STRANDED

ERIC WALTERS

HarperCollins*Publishers*Ltd

http://www.harpercanada.com

HarperCollins books may be purchased for educational, business, or sales
promotional use. For information please write: Special Markets Depart-
ment, HarperCollins Canada, 55 Avenue Road, Suite 2900, Toronto,
Ontario M5R 3L2.

First published in trade paper by HarperCollins in 1998
First mass market edition

Canadian Cataloguing in Publication Data

Walters, Eric, 1957–
Stranded

ISBN 0-00-638592-3

I. Title.

PS8595.A598S87 1999   jC813'.54   C98-930608-9
PZ7.W34St 1999

03 04 OPM 6 5

Printed and bound in the United States

For Snowball, Sammy and Winslow—
and the three children they help to care for.

ACKNOWLEDGEMENTS

I'd like to thank Marie Campbell — for believing
in the original draft . . . and then helping to
make it better.

"Come on, Mom!" I said, stepping back half a step. "Don't embarrass me."

"Embarrass you? What's so embarrassing about your mother trying to give you a hug goodbye? I hug you all the time."

"But not here . . . you know . . . in front of every-body," I quietly pleaded.

"What's the difference? Don't the kids in your class know that your mother loves you and is going to miss you?"

All around us kids were saying goodbye to their parents, joking around with each other and getting themselves and their stuff onto the bus. The sky was dark and it was threatening rain.

"Just give me a handshake," my father suggested, moving closer. He'd been standing just off to the side. I reached out my hand and we shook.

"You understand, don't you, Dad?"

"Of course I do. I wasn't always forty. I remember exactly what it was like to be twelve years old and —"

"That doesn't surprise me," my mother interrupted. "You remembering what *forty* is like, now that would shock me!"

"Well, some people get old before their time and some stay young at heart —"

"And some people can't accept that they're getting older and go through mid-life crisis and start acting like overaged teenagers and think they need a younger wife and —"

"Stop it! Both of you, just stop it. Please! You both promised!" I quietly pleaded through clenched teeth.

I really wanted them both here to see me off so we could act like a real family again. But they just couldn't seem to be polite to each other. They hadn't exchanged more than a few words without fighting for a year before the separation, and living apart for the past eight months hadn't improved the situation.

"You're right, dear, I'm sorry," Mom apologized.

"So am I," my father added.

"Imagine that!" my mother chuckled. "We should make a note of this, the first thing we've agreed on in —"

"Stop!" I said sharply, and she closed her mouth. I looked around and noticed other people had stopped talking and were looking at us.

She nodded her head. "I guess I'm a bit nervous. My little boy is going away."

"It's just for a week, and it's not like I'm going to

be joining the army. It's only a school trip."

"And it is a good way for him to really get to know the kids in his new school," my father chipped in.

"Of course, not the way he'll ever know the children in his last school . . . the school he went to for the first eight years of his education, until circumstances *ripped* him from that school and ..." She paused and gave a satisfied smile. "But I'm getting off topic. I'm sure everything will be fine, just fine."

Mom hardly ever missed a chance to take a shot at Dad. Not that I blamed her. I'd taken more than a couple of shots at him myself. It wasn't her idea, and it certainly wasn't mine, that he leave our house. And it didn't make it any easier to see him driving around town in his new convertible with Amie sitting beside him.

She's unbelievably young — so young she dots her "i"s with little hearts, and when she speaks her voice is so high pitched it sounds like she's inhaling helium. It drives me crazy when she wants to talk music with me and pretend we're "buddies." Of course, it makes more sense for the two of us to be buddies than it does for her to be dating my father, since she's a lot closer to my age than she is to his. There should be some law against that.

I know I wouldn't like it no matter who he was dating, but it's just so embarrassing to see the two of them together — like he's dating my baby-sitter. Of course she's not a baby-sitter — she's a secretary at the hospital where my father works. I can't understand how a smart guy like him can't see how stupid he looks.

I craned my neck so I could see around my father.

In the parking lot, sitting in my father's convertible, sat Amie. It was one of my weekends staying at my father's place so he was the one who dropped me off for the trip. I knew they often drove in to work together, but somehow I'd hoped it would just be the two of us this morning — another wish that didn't come true. Thank goodness she'd stayed put in the car, parked, if not out of sight, at least at a safe distance.

"This is going to be quite a field trip," my father noted. "Seven days and six nights on Sand Spit Island, studying the ocean and ecology. What an adventure!"

"It's going to be neat," I agreed, although I was feeling a little bit nervous, and I think it could be heard in my voice. I'd never slept away from home before, unless you include at my grandparents, and even then it was only for two nights.

"You'll do fine. You know we're just a phone call away," my father offered reassuringly.

"Nope. No telephones."

"No telephones? But that's barbaric!" he objected. "There has to be some way for them to communicate with the mainland if there are problems. What if there's a medical emergency?" My father is a doctor and he's always worried about "medical emergencies."

"They can get help if they need it. The island school is linked to the mainland by a two-way radio. Besides, they're only twenty-five kilometres off the coast. There's nothing to worry about," my mother explained.

"You knew about this?" my father asked.

"Of course . . . and you would have too if you'd taken the time to read the information about the trip that I sent you," she said sharply.

I could tell she was winding herself up to get started on him and I gave her a dirty look, which at least temporarily silenced her.

"Did you pack everything you'll need?" she asked, acting like a mom again.

"Everything." I knew it bothered her that it was my father who had helped me make the final preparations, even though she'd helped me pack my bag before I'd gone to my father's house two nights earlier.

"A housecoat? Slippers? Two bathing suits?"

"Yes, Mom, I brought everything."

"The second bathing suit is important. You may be in the water a lot and there's nothing worse than getting into a wet bathing suit. You can get yourself a bad rash in a place you can't scratch in public, if you get my drift," Mom said.

"Mom!"

"And after the scorching summer we've had, I heard the water is the warmest ever recorded in New England for this time of the year."

"It's a shame the weather is so overcast today," my father noted. "Although the predictions are the storm will peter out down south and the weather will be fair and sunny by tomorrow."

"Thank you very much for the weather report," my mother replied sarcastically. "Now back to the question I asked you and you didn't answer — are you sure you've packed everything?"

"I've got everything," I replied. There was more than a hint of annoyance in my voice.

"That's what your father always said before he went away on his conferences but he was always short on underwear. Did you pack enough underwear? There should be seven pairs for seven days. Here, let me just do a last-minute check," she offered.

Before I could react she'd grabbed my suitcase, placed it on the ground, unsnapped the two buttons and started to open it up. I bent down and pushed both hands against the lid to stop it from opening.

"Mom, please, I don't want you counting my underwear out here in front of everybody."

"Why? They don't know that you wear underwear? Don't any of *them* wear underwear?" She looked like she was going to give me more of an argument, but instead she snapped the locks back into place. "I'm just trying to be a good mother, that's all," she said. She looked hurt, and I thought I could detect a slight tremble in her lower lip, which was the first hint of tears to follow. I knew the signs well . . . it wasn't like I hadn't seen enough tears over the past months to know when they were coming.

"I'm just trying to do the very best for my son," she continued, her voice breaking.

"Mom, I know that," I said. *Please, please don't cry here in front of everybody*, I thought. I reached over and squeezed her hand.

She sniffled a little and seemed to regain her composure. "And it's not like you remembered everything. You forgot to pack one *very* important thing," she said smugly.

"I did? What did I forget?"

"Sammy."

"Sammy ..." I was struck by a terrible thought as she took a bag off her shoulder and handed it to me. "Please don't tell me you packed my . . . my," I lowered my voice, "my teddy bear."

"Yes, I did. When I went upstairs this morning I noticed him snuggled down in your bed. You always sleep better with him so I brought him along. I know you don't always take him to your father's, but I couldn't imagine you going a whole week without him. Should I take him out of the bag for the bus ride in case you want to have a little nap?"

"NO!" I yelled. Again, I looked around and saw that my voice had attracted the attention of other people. "I mean, no thank you," I said, changing my tone so I wouldn't provoke any more tears.

It was true that I did sleep with Sammy almost every night. I used him as more of a pillow than a stuffed animal, but it was also true I didn't want to let everybody in my new school know about my bear. I'd only been in the school three weeks and it was hard enough to get to know people and fit in. It seemed like everybody in the whole school had known everybody else forever and I didn't know anybody. My bear showing up was just what I needed. The few friendships I'd made would sink. First chance I had I'd ditch the bear deep in my suitcase.

My father started making little clucking sounds and slowly shook his head.

"And what exactly is your problem?" my mother demanded.

"What makes you think I have any problem?" he asked.

"I may not be twenty years old, like some people, but I was married to you for almost that long. Don't think I didn't pick up a few things about you. As soon as you start clucking like a chicken I know you're bothered about something."

He stopped clucking. "Well . . ." He hesitated.

"Well what?"

He took a deep breath. "He's twelve years old . . . didn't you think it would be embarrassing for him to have all the kids see him with his teddy bear?"

"Or to hear about it?" I interrupted. "Could you both just keep it down?"

They sheepishly complied.

I knew from experience, lots of experience, that they were on the verge of another full-blown argument. And even if they wanted to stop, they wouldn't be able to once they got started. I'd watch them try to contain themselves but it was like fighting gravity or against magnetic attraction or something, and sooner or later, they would just start into each other.

It was funny, though, no matter how often it happened, I still hoped it wouldn't. I prayed they'd both wake up one day and realize they really should be together and this whole separation thing would just fade away to a bad memory. Things like that happen. I've known kids whose parents have gotten back together. It happens.

"You'd better check in with your teacher," my mother suggested.

"Where is she?" my father asked. "I'd like to meet her."

I looked around. "There's Mrs. Murphy." I pointed. "Standing by the bus door, holding the clipboard."

"Wow! She's awfully old!" my father said.

"Please!" my mother scolded him. "Have you no manners whatsoever?"

My father's face flashed with anger. He hated her to correct him — which is probably why she loved doing it.

"Your teacher isn't that old, is she, dear?" my mother asked me.

"How would I know?"

"This seems like a large group of kids for one teacher to take care of," my father said.

"There's two classes going, both of the seventh-grade classes."

"So there's another teacher as well," my mother added.

"I hope she's a little bit younger," my father said.

"A lot younger. Ms. Fleming . . . that's her beside Mrs. Murphy."

"That's a teacher?" my father exclaimed.

"Yeah. This is her first year teaching," I answered.

"She hardly looks old enough to be a teacher," he observed.

"Oh, don't you worry about that. She is a teacher. She's twenty-three years old. Actually, it's a shame she isn't a few years younger," my mother observed.

"Why is that?" my father asked.

"Well, if she were you could date her . . . oh, but I forgot, you and Annie are going steady or you gave her your class ring or something like that, right?"

"Her name is Amie."

"Annie, Amie, Bunnie or Candie. It makes no difference to me."

My father looked like he wanted to say something, but he thought better of it and just ignored her. Ignoring her always was his best strategy. "I just don't know if there's going to be adequate supervision for this trip. One of your teachers seems too old and the other is far too inexperienced," my father objected. "There should be more supervision."

"Did you even bother to read any of the information about the field trip?" my mother demanded angrily.

"Well, I meant to . . . it's just that I didn't have time . . . I've been very busy at the hospital . . . and . . ."

"Well, it's certainly nice to know some things don't change. If you'd taken the time you would have learned that the island school is staffed by two marine biologists who supervise and coordinate all aspects of the field trip. Supervision is excellent!"

"That's most reassuring, most," he mumbled.

"Hey! Gordo!"

I turned around to see Chuck and Mike, a couple of guys from my school, walking up and waving to me.

"Hi guys."

I caught the look of stunned surprise on my father's face as he looked at the two of them. My mother broke into a pleased grin at his displeasure.

Chuckie was in my class, and of all the kids in the new school he was the one I'd gotten to know best. Mike was in the other class and I didn't know him that well, but I knew a thing or two about him. He was a year older than everybody else because he'd failed a grade. That only partially explained why he was bigger than the other grade sevens — actually, he was bigger than the grade eights. He had a reputation for being able to handle himself, and everybody gave him a lot of space. The few times I'd been around him — he was a friend of Chuckie's and I was just tagging along — he'd made it clear that he didn't care much about me. That was no real surprise, though — with the exception of Chuckie, nobody in the whole school had been overly friendly to me.

They were both different from the type of kids I used to hang around with at my old school. For starters, Chuck had green hair and Mike had none. Second, they both had earrings and dressed casual. My friends at my old school always looked like they were posing for a Sears catalogue. And that was the way I used to dress too. But I'd gotten much more casual — my mom called it sloppy — since school started. You have to try to fit in.

"This is going to be some dynamite trip," Chuck offered.

"For sure," Mike chipped in.

Chuck looked up at my parents. "How you doing today, Mrs. Gordo?"

"I'm fine, Chuckie. And you?" my mother asked.

"Excellent. Just excellent. And is this Mr. Gordo?"

"Mr. Gordo?" my father questioned stiffly. "I'm Gordon's father, Dr. Stevens. Didn't he mention I was a doctor?"

"Nope. Pleased to meet ya, Dr. Gordo," Chuck offered.

My father looked even more indignant and my mother seemed to be working hard not to laugh.

"Are you two going to be sharing a room with Gordon?" she asked.

"For certain," Chuckie answered. "I think they put me in with these two 'cause they like to have somebody responsible in each room. I'll take care of them, don't worry."

"Speaking of worry, did you pack *everything*?" Mike asked Chuckie. "If you know what I mean . . ."

"What *do* you mean?" my father asked suspiciously.

"You know, like socks and shoes and underwear," Mike answered. "Most people don't pack enough underwear. An extra pair for each day of the trip is the rule I live by."

"See?" my mother replied.

"You bring along enough underwear?" Chuckie asked me.

"Yeah, I don't want to share a room with any guy with poor personal hygiene," Mike added.

"Poor personal hygiene?" I wasn't expecting that sort of language out of him. He didn't strike me as too bright.

"Yeah. We learned all about that stuff last year in health class. Health is my favourite subject."

"That's because it's the only subject he does well

in," Chuck chuckled.

"That's not true!" Mike objected.

"Okay, gym and health."

"That's better," Mike agreed.

The sky was looking more ominous by the second. Instead of getting brighter as the morning passed it was actually getting darker. I felt a few drops of rain.

"It does look like it's gonna pour. I heard we're getting the secondary effects of the hurricane that's hitting down south," Mike said.

"Secondary effects? What are you, the weatherman?" Chuck teased.

"No, but I was watching TV last night and they were talking all about it."

"You were watching the news?" Chuck sounded surprised.

"I was waiting for the sports and it came on. What was I supposed to do, plug my ears?"

"Oh, okay," Chuck answered, reassured.

"Boys, if you could excuse us ...?" my father asked, sounding annoyed.

"Oh, yeah, sure. We'll save you a seat on the bus," Chuck offered, and they wandered off through the crowd.

"Yeah, right, a seat," Mike muttered under his breath.

"Nice seeing ya again Mrs. Gordo, take it easy Dr. Gordo."

"Remember Chuckie, you're welcome over to the house any time," my mother said, smiling sweetly. "And you too!" she called to Mike. He didn't reply.

My father watched them walk away. The expression on his face gave a pretty clear message about what he thought of them. "How long have you known those two?" he asked.

"How long could he know anybody? He's only been in the school for three weeks!" my mother answered.

"I met Chuckie on the first day of school."

"They don't seem like your usual sort of friends . . . the sort of friends you had at the old school."

"What do you mean?" I asked, playing dumb.

"Leave him alone," my mother defended. "I don't know the one boy . . . what is the bald one called?" she asked.

"Mike," I answered.

"Yes, I don't know Michael, but the other boy, Chuckie, has been over to the house a few times and he's friendly and polite and eats everything I've offered to him!"

Eating food was very important to my mother. If you liked her food you must like her, and Chuckie always wolfed down whatever she served him and asked for seconds and thirds. I didn't have the heart to tell her I'd heard that when Chuckie was in grade four he used to eat bugs and worms to win bets.

"It's just I expected him to choose friends who were . . . who were more like him," my father said, pointing to a boy standing off to the side by his parents.

My father had pointed out Steven. He did look like the kind of kid my father would want me to hang around with. He dressed well, lived in a nice house, did well in school, was liked by the teachers, and his father was some sort of business executive. He was the kind of kid I used to hang out with. At that instant, Steven looked up and saw me looking at him. He shot me a dirty look. No surprise there — he and his friends had made it clear right at the beginning of the school year that they didn't want to include me in their world, and nothing they'd done since then had led me to believe they'd changed their opinion. But that was okay.

Being "good" and hanging around with the "right kids" at my old school hadn't stopped my family from breaking up — maybe it was time to try something different. I'd had enough of the brainiacs and the preppies. They were either boring or dweebs anyway. Chuck, and what I knew of Mike, were way different from that.

Besides, judging from my father's reaction, Chuckie and Mike made him uneasy, and after all I'd been put through with the separation and the move and everything, it was the least I could do to get back at him a little.

"And don't even think about getting your hair done like either of theirs," my father warned.

"Why not? Lots of kids whose parents separate end up doing things for attention."

"Where did you get a silly idea like that?" my father asked.

"From my therapist," I lied. She'd never said those actual words, but she was always saying one goofy thing or another, and it certainly sounded like something she *would* say.

"Oh, I see," my father mumbled, looking down to study his shoes.

After the separation they'd arranged for me to see a child psychologist to help me deal with the "pain" and "grief" caused by the separation. What a joke — the two of them can't get along, fight, yell, throw things and have to live in separate houses, and *I'm* the one who has a problem. Guess again. Like they really cared what I wanted. If they had, they wouldn't have separated in the first place. They would have grown up and stopped acting like babies. It was a total waste of my time, but I hoped I could somehow get the therapist to convince them that they should get back together, for my sake.

"But what does Chuckie's hair have to do with separation? I thought he lived with both his parents," my mother asked.

"He does. It's just, lots of kids whose parents get divorced do things like that. There's no telling how it affects people is all I'm saying. No telling what can happen . . . no telling," I said, as a sort of warning. I saw those tears start to well up in her eyes again and was hit by a wave of guilt. It seemed like the only time I wasn't feeling angry was when I felt guilty — what a choice.

They both looked a little shook up.

I glanced up at the bus and saw Chuck, hanging halfway out of the bus window, waving to me.

"Perhaps this is a good time for me to meet the teachers who will be in charge of you," my father said.

"Okay," I said.

"Are you coming along?" he asked my mother.

"Me? I was there the first day of school to meet his teacher. I volunteer at the school three mornings a week. I know every teacher in the school. I have time for my son," she said pointedly. "I'll just make sure his bag gets loaded."

"Fine," my father shot back. "Come, Gordon."

When he talked to me in that tone I always expected the next thing he said would be "Sit, Gordon" or "Roll over, Gordon" or "Good boy, Gordon." I trailed after him — "Heel, Gordon."

I introduced my father to Mrs. Murphy and Ms. Fleming.

"Hello, I'm most pleased to meet you. I was just wondering if we could discuss what would happen during a medical emergency. As you're probably aware, I'm a doctor, so this is of concern to me."

I was always amazed at how fast he could work being a doctor into every conversation with new people. I don't know why he couldn't just be my father. I stood there like a piece of lawn furniture while the two teachers tried to explain things to him and he tried to impress them with how smart and wonderful and cool he was.

I looked over to my mother. She was bent over my suitcase. She'd opened it up and the lid blocked my view, but I knew, even without seeing, that she was counting my underwear.

MONDAY 9:15 A.M.

I settled into the seat beside Chuckie's. Right behind us Mike was lying across two seats. He said he needed the extra space because he liked to sit big. The rain was really starting to pelt down now and drops splattered in through the open window. I leaned over top of Chuckie and waved goodbye to my mom. She was one of the few parents still standing there in the rain. Most of the others had run off for shelter or already left for home. Her hair was getting plastered to her head, and with those big, sad eyes of hers she looked like a lost little kitten scratching at the door trying to get in out of a storm. I had to look away.

I hadn't been surprised when my father took off quickly. He'd left the top down on his convertible and didn't want Amie to get wet. I guess she could have put it up herself, but I wouldn't have risked money on her being able to do much of anything on her own. I couldn't figure out what he saw in her . . . scratch that thought . . . other than how she looked, I couldn't figure out what he saw in her.

The bus started into motion and a cheer rose up above the clamor of conversation.

"On the road again!" Chuckie called out, punching me on the arm.

"Ow, that hurt!"

"Settle down, gentlemen."

I looked up to see Ms. Fleming standing in the aisle, almost on top of me. Because she wasn't my teacher I really didn't know her very well. The little I did know came from Mike, or more correctly from Mike having told Chuckie and Chuckie telling me. It wasn't like Mike ever said much to me.

"Don't worry, Ms. Fleming, I'll make sure they don't cause you no grief," Mike said, popping his head over the top of the seat.

"You're taking care of them? Now that's reassuring," she answered sarcastically.

"My pleasure." Obviously Mike hadn't picked up the tone of her voice.

"And you're going to be good too, right Mike?" Ms. Fleming asked.

"Aren't I always?"

"Well ..." she paused. "So far, but I've heard things. Just *stay* good."

She flashed a smile, turned and started back down the aisle for the front of the bus. She really didn't look very old. It wasn't just that she was young but that she was very tiny. Mike was slightly taller and definitely outweighed her. Then again, Mike was taller and bigger than almost everybody.

"Shoot! She's sitting in the front, and I saved her a seat and everything," Mike said.

"Give it up, Mike," Chuckie said.

"No way, she likes me, I can tell."

"'Course she likes you, but do you really think any guy in seventh grade has a chance with his teacher?"

"Hey, hey, don't forget, I'm not just *any* guy in seventh grade," Mike objected.

"Oh, excuse me, I forgot." Chuckie turned to me. "Mike isn't just any guy in seventh grade. He's a guy in seventh grade who's supposed to be in the eighth grade. You know, an older man."

"Older than you, anyway. Besides, it's just a matter of time. She may be a lot older than me now, but in ten years ..." he let the sentence drift off.

"She'll still be a lot older than you," Chuckie argued.

"Yeah, but it's a percentage thing. Right now I'm thirteen and she's twenty-three. She's nearly twice as old as me. In ten years I'll be twenty-three and she'll be thirty-three, which is only one-third older. Ya see, eventually I'll catch up to her."

"Yeah, right. Just like eventually you'll graduate from high school, but I wouldn't want to hang around waiting for that either," Chuckie laughed.

From the back of the bus somebody started up with a chorus of "Ten thousand bottles of beer on the wall."

"All right, my favourite song!" Chuckie cheered.

"This is your favourite song?" I questioned in amazement.

"Sure. It's the only one I know all the words to," he answered, and then he added his voice to the choir.

I closed my eyes. I hadn't got much sleep last night. I never slept very well at my father's — but then who was I fooling, I hadn't been sleeping very well for a long time. I'd lie down in my bed feeling tired and then my mind would just jump to life. I kept having the same thoughts play around in my head, thinking about what had happened and trying to think of some way to make things right — but no matter how often it played out, I couldn't think of the answers.

It was going to be a three-hour bus ride to the docks and I could use the time to sleep. I closed my eyes. I wished I could get Sammy out and snuggle with him.

12:30 P.M.

"Come on, Gordo, wake up. Hurry or you'll miss the boat!"

"What?" I muttered, rubbing my eyes.

"The boat, the boat, hurry or you'll miss the boat! You fell asleep. Hurry!" Mike yelled.

Wide-eyed, I frantically gazed around the bus. Except for the three of us it was completely empty. Chuckie and Mike raced down the aisle. I leaped to my feet, stumbled and fell flat on my face, the wind rushing out of my lungs as I hit the floor.

Chuckie ran back down the aisle. He reached down and offered me a hand. "You okay, man?"

I took a big breath and with Chuckie's help I rose to my feet. I tried to take another step and almost fell to the floor again, landing in Chuckie's out-stretched arms.

Mike started chuckling.

"Gord, check your shoes before you hurt yourself," Chuckie directed.

I looked down. My shoelaces were tied together. "How did that happen?"

"I guess they got all tangled or something when you were sleeping," Mike suggested.

"Or something," Chuckie added.

"Yeah, right. Something for sure," I said angrily, bending down to untie my laces.

"Come on, Gordo, don't be mad. It was just a joke, and we waited until everybody else was off the bus. We didn't make a fool of you in front of everybody," Chuckie reasoned.

"Yeah, just in front of us," Mike added. "Besides, Chuckie said you could take a joke. Haven't you got a sense of humour?" There was a taunting tone to his voice.

I untied the lace and straightened up quickly. "It wasn't that funny, and besides, we don't want to miss the boat. Come on!"

Chuckie put his hands on my shoulders. "The boat doesn't leave for another thirty minutes."

"But you said . . ."

"That was to get you to run."

"The better to make you fall harder," Mike explained.

"It was just a joke," Chuckie explained again. "Besides, I'm sure you'll have a chance to get even before too long."

"Right, a joke." The first few months had been nothing but a big, long joke — on me — and I was getting tired of it. But what could I do?

We climbed down the steps of the bus and into a driving rainstorm. We ran down the side of the bus to the open luggage compartment and grabbed our bags.

"Follow me!" Mike yelled.

We ran after him and into a building. Pushing through the door we found ourselves in a waiting area holding the rest of the kids from our school. Most were sitting down with their luggage. A few were up playing the video games in the corner. Ms. Fleming walked over to where we stood.

"Feeling better?" she asked.

"Um . . . I feel fine." Why was she asking me how I felt?

"The boys said a little bit of sleep would help you get over your bus sickness. That was so considerate of Mike and Chuck. They made everybody leave the bus quietly so you could get a little more rest."

"Very considerate," I muttered under my breath.

"I hope you'll be okay . . . what with this weather, I assume the boat ride will be a lot rougher than the bus."

"I'll be fine." Rough water didn't bother me. One of the casualties of the separation was that my father had had to sell his boat. I really missed that boat — and the good times the three of us had on it.

"Good! Now I'd better go and find out what's happening," she said.

She left us and went over to where Mrs. Murphy was standing with some man.

"You two are lucky I don't get seasick."

"Why?" Chuckie asked.

"Because if I did I'd make sure, really sure, to hurl right on the two of you."

"He's the one who tied your laces together!" Chuckie replied, pointing at Mike.

"Way to stick together, Chuck," Mike said.

"Attention, please! Attention!"

The noise in the room faded away and all eyes turned to Ms. Fleming, who was standing on a chair. On a chair beside her stood the man Mrs. Murphy had been talking to. Mrs. Murphy sat over to the side. She looked tired.

"Gather round!" she yelled.

"Big voice for a little person," Chuckie observed.

"That's nothing. You should hear her when somebody gets her mad," Mike added. "Not that *I've* ever got her mad." Both of them started to chuckle.

We shuffled over with the other kids and surrounded her.

"I'd like you all to meet one of the people who will be charge of our field trip. This is Dr. Resney."

"Thank you, Ms. Fleming. The boat to take us to the island has arrived. It's normally a sixty-minute ride, however, due to the storm, it will take over ninety minutes and feel a lot longer. The waves are high . . . very high. We're going to be riding two metre swells out there."

There was a buzz of conversation and nervous laughter behind the conversation. I'd never been out in waves that big before.

"But . . ." he started loudly, and everybody shut up to listen. "There is nothing to worry about. The boat is designed to handle much rougher seas than this little blow."

"It's going to be just like a really long roller coaster ride," Ms. Fleming chipped in.

Kids cheered in response. Not me though. I hate roller coasters.

"Please, everybody get their bags and assemble by the doors to the dock," Ms. Fleming ordered.

She jumped off the chair and walked over to where Mike, Chuckie and I stood.

"Boys, do you think you could take your bags and give me an extra hand with my things?"

"Sure!" Mike answered for all of us. It was pretty obvious that he had a crush on her. He reminded me of the way my father acted around Amie.

"Thanks. They're right over there in the corner," she said, pointing to the far side of the room. "And be careful with the oxygen tanks. They're heavy, and the valve is very delicate."

"Oxygen tanks?" I asked.

"Yeah, I brought along my scuba equipment. I hope I can do some diving. I dove with some dolphins off the coast of Florida this summer."

"Wow, that sounds neat!" Mike said enthusiastically.

"It was incredible! Just incredible! And I hear the waters off this island hold dozens of different types of dolphins and whales. I'd love to have that experience again."

"That would be amazing," Mike said.

"We'll all keep our fingers crossed and hope for the best," she said, flashing a big smile. "Thanks for getting my stuff. I'll see you three on board."

1:15 P.M.

The boat was big, but the ocean was much, much bigger. We dashed across the rain-swept dock. Boarding was tricky, especially carrying the extra things for Ms. Fleming, but we managed to negotiate the shifting gangplank and took our seats with the rest of the kids inside the vessel.

I looked out the window and watched the shore rise up, up, up and up . . . and then sink down, down, down and down. My stomach seemed to be travelling in the exact opposite direction from the way the boat was being carried. This was stupid. I'd never got seasick before.

I hoped it would get better once the boat left the dock, but instead it seemed to get worse as we travelled. This was turning out to be the longest ninety minutes of my life. It didn't help to pass the time by talking because nobody seemed to be in any mood to talk. I turned my eyes away from the window. Chuckie and Mike sat with their eyes trained on the floor. I tapped Chuckie on the leg. He looked up and gave me a weak smile. Then he burped, groaned and bent over. I grabbed the seat ahead of me and struggled to my feet. I'd only taken a few steps when I heard the unmistakable gagging sound signalling Chuckie was "up-chucking." I stumbled along between the rows of seats, bumping into half a dozen kids with their heads in their laps. I heard more gagging, coming from the opposite direction from where Chuckie was sitting. The pungent scent of vomit filled the air.

I moved to the back of the lounge. I needed to get to a washroom. The boat rocked and I was thrown into a wall. Luckily my hands absorbed the impact. I could feel my feet slip and I worked to regain my balance. I lurched to the washrooms. Both were occupied and kids were waiting to get inside. This wasn't going to work.

I looked past the washrooms. There was another door at the end of the corridor and it led to the deck. Mrs. Murphy had made it clear we were to stay inside the lounge and not go up top, but I didn't care. I'd rather risk getting her mad than embarrass myself by losing my breakfast in front of all these kids I hardly knew. Somehow vomiting wouldn't help them to think of me as any more "cool" than they did now. Besides, a little fresh air could only help.

I took off down the corridor and pushed against the door just as the boat pitched to one side. I was thrown out, and rolled along the deck until I smashed into the railing. I picked myself up and looked over in time to see the door to the lounge slam shut. A wave broke just in front of me and the water splashed down and washed along the deck, soaking me along one side before it rolled back under the railing and into the ocean. I struggled to my feet. There was a roof overhanging the deck which offered some protection from the driving rain. Still, it couldn't stop the winds from pushing enough rain and spray underneath to start soaking the rest of me. Maybe I wanted some fresh air, but not this much.

I lunged for the door and grabbed the handle. It turned, but the door wouldn't open. It was locked! I pounded my fist against it. The sound seemed to be lost in the roar of the wind and waves. I pressed my face against the glass. Nobody heard me or even glanced my way.

This wasn't working either. I'd have to circle around and come back in through the front doors. I held on firmly to the railing and pulled myself forward. Along with the rain, the wind was whipping up spray off the tops of the waves. I couldn't help but think about what would happen to anybody who fell overboard. The boat pitched forward again and I fell to my knees. I hauled myself back up and kept moving.

I tried to keep my eyes aimed straight ahead but I couldn't help but look out at the waves again. I couldn't believe how big they were! I took a deep breath and doubled my resolve to get back inside. Once I'd turned the corner, I was in the home stretch.

"What are you doing out here?"

I jumped backwards and stumbled over my feet, regaining my balance at the last second.

"Nice move. You must be dynamite on the dance floor." It was Christina, a girl from my class. She was sitting on a large coil of rope with her back against a bulkhead. "You'd better sit down before you break something."

I flopped down beside her. There was a slight overhang, and because of the direction of the wind we were protected from the elements.

"What are you doing out here?" I asked.

"Same as you, avoiding inside." She turned and looked at me, hard. "You're not planning on getting sick out here are you? Because if you are, you have to leave!"

"No, I feel okay!" I protested, and realized that I did feel fine. The air had chased away the sick feelings.

"I just figured anybody who gets bus sick would—"

"I don't get bus sick! That was just Chuckie and Mike . . ."

"I thought they must be playing some sort of joke on you. The last thing in the world those two would ever be is thoughtful."

I nodded my head.

"That's just like them. What did they do?"

"They tied my shoelaces together when I fell asleep on the bus."

"Bad mistake. Never, ever fall asleep around those two."

"Never?"

"Never, ever," she said.

"Boy, am I in trouble."

"How come?" she asked.

"They're my roommates. They have six more shots at me."

"You *are* in trouble . . . unless . . ."

"Unless what?" I asked.

"Unless you can convince them to go after somebody

else. Either you're with them or you're one of their victims," she explained.

"That makes sense. It sounds like you know them pretty well."

"A whole lot better than I want to. Chuckie's been in my class almost every year since kindergarten. And if that isn't a Chuckie overload all by itself, he seems to eat every second meal at my house."

I knew that she and Chuckie were pretty friendly, but I had no idea. She just seemed far too smart and pretty and, well . . . normal, to hang out with him. She was tall and thin and had longish brown hair. She dressed pretty casual and most times I'd seen her she was wearing a rep soccer jacket, which she was wearing now. The jacket had an eagle on the back holding a soccer ball in its talons. She and a couple of other girls, who had the same jacket, were always out at recess kicking around a ball.

"Why does Chuckie eat at your house?" I asked.

"Believe me, it isn't my idea. He lives next door. My parents like him, though, and my brother keeps inviting him, so I'm stuck with Chuck."

"Your brother? Who's your brother?"

"Mike."

"Mike? Mike is your brother?"

"Yep."

"But you don't look like . . ."

"I guess I would if I shaved my head," she chuckled. "Everybody knows we're brother and sister, although there have been times when I wish nobody knew."

I wanted to ask her why her brother didn't seem to like me, but I didn't know her well enough to ask.

"Look, there's the island!" Christina yelled

I glanced up and saw the dark shape of the land looming in front of us. As I watched, a flare of light burst in my eyes and then swept off to the side. There was a lighthouse on the island. It was still midday but the rain and cloud had blocked the sun so completely it looked like early evening.

As the beam of light spun around and caught my eye again I thought about all the stories I'd ever read about the sea and islands and lighthouses. Those stories were always filled with adventure. I didn't want an adventure. All I wanted was to be dry.

"We'd better get inside and get our stuff," I suggested. I tried to get to my feet but Christina placed a hand on my shoulder, holding me in place.

"Stay here. Inside is going to be awful. Wall to wall puke. Besides, if you go in now the teachers will know you were outside. Wait until they let the rest of the kids come on deck and they'll never notice you weren't there."

I settled back into the seat. What she was saying made perfect sense. As she sat staring straight ahead I tilted my head so I could see her. She had soft, gentle blue eyes. Her hair was tied in a pony-tail. Of course I'd noticed her before — it's hard not to notice somebody who sits two seats ahead of you all day — but I'd never really looked at her. Suddenly she turned toward me and our eyes met. I turned my eyes away in embarrassment.

Coming closer to the island the boat turned to the right, or I guess the starboard side, and paralleled the shore. When we were on my dad's boat he always insisted we use the correct nautical terms. Anybody using words like right or left or front or back was threatened with walking the plank.

The beacon of light from the lighthouse swirled around, sweeping over us with every rotation. After travelling alongside the shore for a few minutes we turned hard to starboard, straight for the land.

"We're heading into a little bay," Christina observed.

I stood up to get a better look. We were passing through a small gap of water between two fingers of land.

I heard the slap of feet on the deck and pressed my back into the shelter to get out of view as much as possible. Within a few seconds a crew member appeared at the bow of the boat and started to uncoil some ropes.

"Come on, kids, time to move," a second sailor said, appearing out of nowhere.

I was so startled I practically jumped to my feet.

"Didn't mean to scare you, son," the sailor apologized. "Especially in front of your girlfriend."

"My girlfriend? But she's not my girlfriend!" I objected.

"No, you have it wrong," Christina said, rising to her feet. "We were just talking!"

"Sure thing, whatever you say," he answered, winking at me broadly. "How old are you two, anyway?"

"Twelve," we answered in unison.

STRANDED

"Twelve. I remember my first girlfriend, Carol Lubka. It seems like only —"

"She's not my girlfriend!"

"Sure, kid, whatever you say."

He grabbed the end of the coil of rope we'd been sitting on and dragged it toward the railing. We were coming quickly into shore. There were gigantic tires spaced along a dock to cushion the impact of the boat. We bumped into touch and two sailors leaped over the side, towing the lines with them. They looped the ropes along the pylons to secure the boat. The boat was thrown against the dock a second time and I lost my footing. Christina reached out to try and grab me and I fell into her arms.

"What are you two doing?"

We both turned around to see Ms. Fleming standing at the now open door to the lounge. A bunch of kids, bags in hand, were standing all around her.

"We were just . . . I was falling . . ." I stammered as we disentangled ourselves from each other.

Kids broke into smiles and chuckles. Thank goodness I couldn't see either Chuckie or Mike among them.

I felt myself blush. "But . . ."

"Please, can I have your attention!" Dr. Resney called out, and all the attention swung around to him. He was climbing down the ladder from the bridge.

I didn't care what he was going to say, I was just grateful he was the centre of attention now. Everyone stopped and looked at him.

"Everyone must leave the boat immediately!" he shouted.

· 33 ·

All the noise that wasn't being generated by the waves and wind stopped.

"The waves are getting much bigger and they're affecting the sand bars. The gap leading into this little bay has been narrowed by almost six metres since I went through there this morning. The captain is afraid if the boat doesn't leave soon it'll be trapped or run aground on the sand. It has to get back to the shelter of the harbour quickly!"

Mrs. Murphy stood there silently. She nodded her head slowly in acknowledgment.

"All right, everybody proceed in an orderly manner, walking in threes with your roommates. I will have no shoving or pushing or you will be returning with this boat to the mainland. Do I make myself clear?"

There was a mumble of responses.

"Do I make myself clear?" she asked in a much louder voice, easily rising to a level that almost silenced the storm.

"Yes ma'am," people replied.

"Good. Now, Dr. Resney, please lead the way and we will follow."

The crowd started to move forward. Christina and I had to go against the current, back into the lounge to get our bags. On the way we ran into Mike and Chuckie. They both looked worse for wear.

"Some ride," Chuckie noted.

"Yeah, what happened to you?" Mike asked, completely ignoring his sister, who proceeded to the far side to get her things. I watched her and noticed that she and Mike had pieces from the same set of matching luggage.

"I went outside to get some air," I answered.

"Good plan. This place was like a rocking barf bowl," Chuckie said.

"Yeah, I can tell. Anyone with a nose would have known that."

"We saved you the trouble of puking up on us," Mike mentioned, motioning down to his stained running shoes. "These are practically new. I hope they wash out okay."

I stifled a laugh. Between his stained shoes, sloped shoulders and green face, Mike didn't seem so big and tough.

"Come on guys, shake a leg!" Christina yelled from the door.

"I don't even want to think about shaking anything," Chuckie replied quietly.

I bent down and picked up my bag. Something dripped off the bottom corner and I felt my stomach shudder.

"Sorry, man," Mike apologized.

I grabbed Ms. Fleming's other bag and we all started for the exit. By the time we reached the door the only other person still on board, Christina, was being helped onto the dock. We hurried over and two sailors practically flung our luggage dock side. Then they grabbed me by the arms and helped me off the boat. No sooner had our feet touched the dock than the sailors released the ropes, the boat's engines roared, and it inched away from the wharf.

"Wow, they weren't wasting any time," Chuckie said.

"I can't blame them. I want to get in out of this weather too," Mike responded. He turned the collar up on his jean jacket

"Come on, let's get going," Chuckie suggested, and he and Mike started to move.

The rest of the class was snaking along a path that wound its way from the dock up to a building a few hundred metres away. It sat on the top of a rocky cliff. A dim light shone through a few of the windows, cutting through the darkening skies. It was only 2:45 in the afternoon, but the sky looked like it was dusk. The rain was pelting down and, with the force of the wind propelling it, the drops stung as they hit my face. I set down my bag and looked up at the line of kids, carrying their luggage, bumping along the path away from the docks, pushing through the rain. I couldn't help but think about how hesitant I was to come on this trip in the first place and how badly things had started. I wished I was back at home — and then remembered that the home I was wishing for didn't even exist any more. I picked up my bag and started up the hill.

MONDAY 3:00 P.M.

It felt good to get in out of the rain and I dropped the bags to the floor. All around me kids were breaking into little groups of four, or five, or six kids and sitting in the chairs encircling the dozens of tables filling the room. I felt exposed standing there by myself. I would have liked to have walked up to one of the groups and joined in, but I didn't feel that I could. Where was Chuckie?

Despite being inside I still felt chilly. I was soaked right through to the bone. The room was dimly lit. Hanging from the ceiling, strategically placed, were about a dozen oil lamps. There were banks of fluorescent lights along the ceiling but they weren't turned on. I guessed they were trying to go for atmosphere. The light thrown off by the oil lamps was bright enough but it had a yellowish tinge to it.

Ms. Fleming, Mrs. Murphy and Dr. Resney stood

off to the side at the front of the hall, all huddled together talking. Dr. Resney broke off and moved to the centre of the room.

"Hello, everybody!" he yelled out.

All the little clusters of kids stopped talking and turned their attention to the front.

"I'd like everybody to take a seat," he continued.

I looked around, unsure where to sit, until I saw Chuckie waving at me. I sat down beside him. Mrs. Murphy raised her hands for silence and we all complied.

"Welcome to Sand Spit Marine School," Dr. Resney said. "I'm sorry your first few hours have been so rough, but I promise you things will get better over the course of your stay. We'll be studying the bird populations that nest on this island and exploring the marine life in the shallows and tidal pools. A highlight for me personally is an examination of the marine mammals in the area, which include seals, sea lions, dolphins and whales."

"Wow, are there really whales?" somebody asked loudly.

"Yes," Dr. Resney responded. "There are more types of whales in this area than off any other coast in North America, and perhaps anywhere in the world. Within the last two weeks we've had confirmed sightings of humpbacks, right whales, bottle-nosed dolphins, long-finned pilot whales and a possible sighting of a young blue whale."

"All of those were seen from shore?" Mrs. Murphy asked.

"All except the blue. The rest frequent the shallows of the island. The dolphins and pilot whales have been chasing schools of mackerel that come into shallower waters this time of year. I'll be shocked if we don't see either a pod of pilot whales or dolphins this week. Both tend to herd schools of fish against the shore. It's incredible to watch the level of coordination involved in their hunting techniques. I'm sure you'll have that opportunity. But before I go into any more detail I think it best you all be assigned to your rooms. I want you to go there, change your clothes, settle in and reassemble in this hall in twenty minutes. Then I can introduce you to the other staff and discuss our present circumstances. Your teachers will now give you your room assignments. Until you are called, remain silently in your seats. Thank you!"

There was a rumbling of conversation.

"I can wait as long as you can. If you would rather chatter like squirrels then change into dry clothes, so be it," Mrs. Murphy stated loudly as she stood up.

Evil glances were cast around the room to silence the few offenders. Everybody wanted to change.

Ms. Fleming called out the first group of three. A triad of kids gratefully rose to their feet and were directed down one of two corridors leading off the dining hall. She called another group, and another. It didn't take long to figure out the pattern: girls down one corridor, boys down the other. Our names were called out. We picked up our bags and walked over to Ms. Fleming.

"Thank you boys for carrying my extra things,"

she said. "Just leave them outside my room. It's marked 'staff,' and it's just down that hall," she said, pointing to the boys' corridor. "And you three are in room . . . let me see . . . here it is . . . room eight."

"My lucky number," Mike beamed.

We walked along the corridor, leaving the scuba tanks, gear and extra bag by the closed "staff" door. I turned and saw the number 8 affixed to the door directly across from Ms. Fleming's.

"I guess we're going to be Ms. Fleming's neighbours," I said.

"Neighbours! No way," Chuckie declared. "This is way too close. Come on, we're going to settle in at the end of the corridor, by the exit doors."

"But Chuckie, this is the room we were assigned," I protested, following after him.

"We were? You're wrong, Gordo, Ms. Fleming assigned us to room two."

"No, she said room eight." I turned to Mike. "Isn't that right, Mike? Room eight, your lucky number."

"My lucky number is eleven."

Mike bumped by me in the narrow corridor and followed after Chuckie. I was speechless, but I had no choice but to follow. I passed by a number of open doors. Dim light, loud laughter and conversations leaked out into the corridor from each room. Up ahead Chuckie and Mike turned into a room. I stood at the open door. There were already three kids in the room, and it looked very crowded with the five of them and their luggage littering the floor.

"No, *we're* in room two," I heard Mike say loudly.

"But room eight is still available," Chuckie added.

"It's closer to the dining room and the washrooms," Mike said.

I knew two of the guys who were already in the room. They were in our class, while the third was in Mike's. They grumbled a little about already being settled in, but when Mike offered to help them relocate both their bags and their butts into the hall they decided to agree to the change. As they walked out the door they all shot me dirty looks, like it was my fault or something. I wanted to apologize or explain, but it wouldn't have done any good.

I went into the room. It was tiny but tidy. There was a small oil lamp, just like the ones in the dining hall, suspended from the ceiling. There was a dresser and a desk, underneath a window. On one wall was a single bed while a bunk bed was against the other.

Chuckie and Mike were arguing about who was going to get the single bed. They both tried to lay claim to it by throwing their bags on the covers. I wasn't in the mood to argue. I tossed my bag onto the top bunk and climbed up. They stopped arguing and looked up at me.

"You can't sleep there," Chuckie protested.

"I'm not moving," I replied. I figured it would be more difficult for them to play any jokes on me in my sleep up there.

Chuckie and Mike exchanged looks. "I'm not sleeping below him," Mike announced.

"Me neither!"

"What's the problem with sleeping in the bunk

ERIC WALTERS

underneath me?" I questioned. "I don't wet my bed, you know."

They both started giggling until the giggling became out and out laughter.

"What's so funny?"

"Well . . . I guess we can all agree you won't wet your bed . . . right, Mike?" Chuckie asked.

"Yeah, deal. Gordo won't wet the bed this trip."

"What are you two talking about?"

"We've just made an agreement that whoever sleeps in the bottom bunk doesn't have to worry about getting a midnight shower, that's all," Chuckie explained.

"Enough of this chitchat. Let's get changed and get back to the dining room," Mike interrupted. "We'll figure out who gets the bed tonight. Maybe we can take turns or something."

Quickly we all opened our bags and grabbed dry clothing. I glanced over my shoulder, and noticing that both Chuckie and Mike were occupied getting their things, I pulled Sammy out of the overnight bag and stuffed him deep into my suitcase.

As soon as we were changed we left the room and Mike closed the door behind him. I started to walk toward the dining room but stopped when I realized that Chuckie and Mike had gone the other way. Chuckie opened the door at the end of the hall and went outside. The door closed behind him and he was framed by the glass. He rattled the doorknob but it wouldn't turn.

"Come on, let me in!" he called out, his voice muffled by the door.

"Should we let him?" Mike asked. "Or should we make him walk around to the front and get soaked again?"

"Come on, I'm getting wet!" Chuckie demanded, pounding on the glass with his fist.

"Okay, okay," Mike said, pushing the door open.

Chuckie surged through the opening. He was wet but not soaked.

"Why did you do that?" I asked.

"Let him in?" Mike questioned.

"No . . . I was talking to Chuckie," I explained. "Why did you go outside?"

"I wanted to see if it locked from the outside. That's important to know. Sneaking out through that door's okay, but we're going to have to jam the lock somehow if we want to go back in the same way."

"But why would we . . .? No, forget it . . . I don't want to know," I said. I turned and walked toward the dining room.

3:50 P.M.

We were among the last to reassemble. We took three seats in the back. I looked around for Christina. I was hoping she could give me some warning about what to expect from my roommates. I needed to know what they were planning.

I didn't see Christina but I noticed two women I didn't know sitting at a table at the front between Ms. Fleming and Mrs. Murphy. Dr. Resney, who was standing beside one of the women, walked to the centre of the room.

"I want to start off," Dr. Resney began, and the room became silent, "by saying we are in no danger whatsoever."

That didn't sound like a very encouraging way to start any discussion. His tone of voice reminded me of my parents' when they gave me that wonderful "we still love you even though we don't love each other any more" speech before Dad moved out of the house.

"Despite the forecast of the National Weather Service, we are experiencing much more than simply the ripple effects of Hurricane Patrick. It was predicted that it would lose speed and strength as it moved over the colder waters, but this hasn't happened. Instead, Patrick, which was downgraded to a tropical storm, has continued to pack quite a punch. As well, rather than heading inland in the Carolinas, it has been parallelling the coast, and the newest guestimate is that it will hit the coast less than a hundred kilometres from us. We are now feeling the effects of one arm of the storm pinwheeling out from the eye."

"Shouldn't we move inland, away from the water?" somebody asked. "I used to live in Florida, and we always moved inland when there was a hurricane."

"You're certainly right," Dr. Resney agreed. "But you must remember, this storm is no longer a hurricane, just a tropical storm, and the reality is that we have no inland to move to. The widest part of this island is less than two kilometres across."

"Why don't we just go back to the mainland?" Mike suggested.

"We can't do that. Crossing over to the mainland is much, much more dangerous than staying put right here. This school, which is a former whaling station, is constructed of brick and cinder blocks. And, while almost all of this island is sand and low to the water, this spot on which you sit is nearly six metres above sea level and built on solid rock. In fact, this location and the lighthouse, on the opposite end of the island, are the only two solid spots. Both acted as the anchors on which sand was deposited to form this island."

"So we are completely safe," Mrs. Murphy said, although I wasn't sure if she was making a statement or asking a question.

"Completely safe. The storm will not cause us to be endangered as much as inconvenienced, starting with the soaking from the rain, the rough ride from the swells and our generator going out, resulting in no electricity for the lights."

That explained all the oil lamps. I'd thought they were just being cute.

"And of course since our stoves are all electric we won't have any hot food available until the generator is fixed, which hopefully should be sometime tomorrow."

There was a wave of grumbling and complaining. I shook my head in amazement; nobody complained about being trapped on a little spit of sand in the middle of a hurricane, but now they were upset because their hot chocolate would have to be cold. Behind the voices were the steady sounds of the wind whistling and the rain driving down against the windows.

"And a final note. It appears the worst of the storm has already passed. According to the latest marine weather forecast we might even experience sunny skies by midday tomorrow."

"Are they the same people who predicted we wouldn't get the storm at all?" Chuckie asked to a chorus of laughter.

"Yes, I'm afraid so," Dr. Resney replied. "Before going any further, I feel I have been negligent in not introducing the remainder of the staff. On the far left is our cook, Mrs. Presley."

The older woman sitting at the end rose to her feet and took a bow.

"And next to her is our other marine biologist, my wife, Tina Resney." The other woman took to her feet.

"Wow, talk about whales!" Chuckie said really loud, which led to a fair bit of twittering from the kids.

Dr. Resney broke into a smile. "And for those of you who haven't guessed, my wife and I are pregnant."

"Correction," she said. "My husband and I are not pregnant . . . only one of us is carrying around a baby. He's just going to become a father."

"We're due . . . I mean, my wife is due in five weeks. This group is very fortunate to have her here. After this week she will be taking an early maternity leave. This island is somewhat isolated and we are unprepared for an unexpected delivery, so she will be remaining at our home on the mainland."

"Thank goodness she's five weeks away from

delivering. She looks like she might pop right here tonight," Chuckie whispered.

"Five weeks isn't much," Mike commented. "My sister was born five weeks early."

"Christina?" I asked.

"Yeah. Only sister I have," he answered.

"So tonight we'll be eating a light supper," Dr. Resney said.

"Light, as in sandwiches, fruit and cheese," Mrs. Presley added.

"Followed by a study session on hurricanes and tropical storms. Then I'm afraid we'll have to turn in fairly early. We don't have much oil for the lamps and we have to conserve what we have by turning them off quite soon."

Right on cue one of the lamps flickered and then faded away to nothing.

"I guess that one just ran out of oil, but as my father used to say to me, 'when all you have is lemons, you should make lemonade.'"

"We only have lemons?" Chuckie questioned.

"No, that's not what he means," Mike replied.

"Since we're on an isolated island in the middle of a storm with no electricity and very little light, we have the perfect place for one thing . . . ghost stories," Dr. Resney said.

6:30 P.M.

We'd been assigned supper seats. Six of us to a table. All the other tables except ours were either all girls or all boys. Mike, Chuckie and I had to share with Christina and her two partners. Neither Mike nor Christina was very happy about it; "I thought I'd get a break from the two stooges," Christina had said loudly. Chuckie had answered with an amazingly loud burp. He said it was one of his "talents." A couple of times during the meal I found myself looking over at Christina. She was laughing and talking to her friends. She seemed so comfortable — so different than how I felt.

I wasn't much interested in supper, although it did kind of remind me of being home. At least, at one of my homes. When I was staying with my father we ate either take-out or one of his three specialties: cold cereal, sandwiches, and soup. These were his versions of breakfast, lunch, and dinner. Actually, a hot bowl of vegetable soup would have gone down pretty good.

9:40 P.M.

After the study session, we gathered again for the evening's entertainment. The first few ghost stories were pretty tame stuff. The usual missing arm, rise from the dead, scream-out-the-punchline stories that everybody knew.

I had to admit, though, that even these lame stories were made at least a little scary by where we were. The oil lights had been extinguished one by one until only two small lamps remained lit. The corners of the room were hidden in the shadows. Outside the rain was still falling, although it seemed to have let up a little. Occasional flashes of lightning lit up the night sky. I knew if

I were an axe murderer, this would be the time and place I'd pick — a bunch of kids trapped on an island in the middle of a hurricane, no way off and no one to rescue them. I'd wait till they went to bed and then kill them, one by one, as they lay sleeping in their beds . . .

"We'll take a short break for a snack before we continue with our stories," Mrs. Murphy announced. "The line forms to my immediate right."

I joined a queue of kids leading up to the table where Mrs. Presley had stacked the snacks. There was a pile of fruit and hunks of cheese. I picked up a paper plate from the end of the table and put a couple of pieces of each on my plate.

I noticed Christina was only a few places behind me in line. I took my time and let Chuckie and Mike head back to our seats. She picked out her stuff and I casually sauntered over.

"Not too scary," I began. My mouth felt dry and the words didn't come out very well.

"Not at all, but you have to remember that I live with Mike," she chuckled.

"I guess you have a point. Could I ask you a question?" I surprised myself — I didn't think I'd find the nerve.

"Of course."

"And I know it probably won't make too much sense," I apologized.

"I'm used to that as well," she said.

"Mike and Chuckie were babbling about not wanting to sleep in the bunk underneath me . . . I just don't understand what they were going on about." I felt embarrassed mentioning any of this to anybody, let alone a girl, but I needed an answer more than I needed my dignity. And besides, she did seem awfully easy to talk to. "Do you have any idea what they were talking about?"

She started laughing, and a couple of the other girls looked at us funny.

"Those jerks," she said, shaking her head. "Come on over here and I'll explain it."

I followed her away from the cluster of kids and over to a darkened corner of the room.

"They were going to wait until you fell asleep and then put one of your hands in a bowl of warm water."

"Why would they want to do that?" I asked.

"To see what would happen next."

"What would happen?" This was confusing.

"A lot could happen. Usually if you do that to somebody it makes them, you know, relieve themselves," Christina said, looking down at the floor.

"Come on, no way that can work," I objected.

"Believe me, it works!"

"You mean . . .?"

She slowly nodded her head. Now she looked embarrassed. "Twice. What jerks. They probably did it to each other a dozen times when one would sleep over at the other's house. The first one to fall asleep would get the treatment. I think they'd still be doing it to each other if my father hadn't made them stop."

"I can see where it would get him mad."

"You don't know the half of it. They got tired of tormenting each other, and me, so they did it to my dad."

"Your dad?"

"Yep. I thought he was going to kill them. I bet he would have except he had to stop to change his PJs." She got a strange look on her face. "But please don't tell anybody about this . . . not about my father . . . and especially not about me." She put her hands on my shoulders. "Promise me, please!"

"Of course I won't tell anybody," I answered.

"Gordon and Christina!"

We both turned to face Ms. Fleming.

"I know about being young and discovering the opposite gender . . ."

"But we're not young!" I protested. "I mean, we're not discovering anything!"

"Honestly," Christina added. Quickly she removed her hands from my shoulders.

"Come back and join the others, the stories are about to begin again. The three of us will sit down and talk about this in the morning," she said.

What choice did we have, about anything? We trailed behind her out of the darkness to rejoin the kids. A few girls giggled as we came into sight. I kept my eyes trained on the floor, glancing up just enough to find my way back to Mike and Chuckie. They hadn't even noticed me being gone and were arguing about who would win in a fight between Godzilla and a giant version of the pink battery bunny.

"As we discussed, it will soon be bedtime," Mrs. Murphy announced to the crowd. This was met by a hail of booing. "But first, Dr. Resney has offered to tell us one more story."

MONDAY 10:15 P.M.

"I must warn everybody that what I'm going to say isn't really a story . . . a story implies make-believe . . . what I'm going to tell you really happened . . . here on this very island . . . almost one hundred years ago."

"Mrs. Murphy was just a little girl a hundred years ago," Chuckie whispered. I almost laughed out loud but stopped myself in time. Did this guy really think anybody was going to get too worked up about his "true story"?

"A time of sailing ships and oil lamps. Does anybody know what they used to fuel those lamps?" Dr. Resney asked.

People mumbled but no one volunteered an answer.

"Whale oil. The lamps were filled with oil derived from the blubber of whales. The blubber from a great whale, a blue or a humpback, could be boiled down and produce hundreds of barrels of oil. Every ship in

Roger's Harbor was a whaling ship, and every man in every house was a whaler. They'd set to sea in their ships, sometimes for weeks at a time, leaving behind their families, to wait and hope and pray for the safe return of their menfolk. Whaling was a hazardous trade and they all knew the dangers well. If the whales, some as big as forty elephants, didn't smash their small wooden boats to splinters, there was the constant danger of the sea. Storms blew up, with hurricane-force winds and waves three times as tall as the little houses in which they lived . . . of course, you'd all know about that, wouldn't you?"

I thought back to the crossing we'd experienced early in the day. I could imagine just how terrifying it might be out there on the ocean. My stomach still felt a little uneasy thinking about my few minutes bouncing around on the open deck.

"Hundreds of ships came to rest on the bottom of the ocean. The waters all around this island are littered with wrecks."

"Excuse me, Dr. Resney, but are any of those wrecks accessible to divers?" Ms. Fleming asked.

"Yes, many of them are. Before the week is over I'm sure you'll have a chance to explore a few."

"Thank you . . . oh, I'm sorry, I didn't mean to interrupt your story, please go on."

Dr. Resney smiled. "So the people of Roger's Harbor decided they needed a lighthouse. They brought over cinder blocks and mortar and wood and built a tower. And on the top of that tower they used glass and special polished lenses and mirrors to reflect the light and send it far out to sea, to warn the ships as well as to lead them to the safety of the harbour. Our present lighthouse is built on the same site, using some of the original blocks and beams.

"Of course there are some differences. Today, it's run almost completely by automation. Whenever the skies darken, a powerful electric spotlight sweeps across the sky, rotating around and around, all pre-programmed and controlled by radio from the mainland.

"Back in those days things were different. Every lighthouse needed a keeper. It was usually a man, often with his family, who lived in a house by the lighthouse. It was lonely and hard work. The keeper had to make sure the lamp stayed lit and the turntable kept the light revolving all through the night.

"Now that they had a lighthouse, the villagers needed to secure a keeper. There was a great deal of discussion and disagreement about who might fill that role. It was suggested that one of the villagers, Captain Amos, should be approached. Some thought he would be too proud to accept the position, given that he'd been the captain of his own ship before, while others thought he wouldn't be up to the hard work involved. You see, the Captain was missing a leg, and one arm hung limp and useless by his side."

He paused and took a sip from his mug. The only sound came from the rain against the roof and windows. I had to admit that, despite my reservations, he'd captured my attention, and judging from the silence around me, most of the others were caught up in the story as well.

"This school is from down state, right?" Dr. Resney asked.

"Yes, that's right," Mrs. Murphy answered.

"Then none of you would know anything about Captain Amos, would you?"

A collection of voices agreed.

"Well, the Captain is famous — or perhaps I should say infamous — around these parts. Let me tell you all about him. At one time he was one of the most respected whaling captains around. He pushed his crews hard and took chances. Some would say too hard, and he took too many chances, but no one could match his success. To be part of his crew was a guarantee of a rich haul, because each crew member was given a percentage of the catch. An empty hold meant an empty stomach for you and your family.

"One stormy fall day there was a report of big blue whales just up the coast. The other captains decided to wait out the weather, but not Captain Amos. Some of the members of his crew didn't want to go, but he threatened and cajoled and challenged them until they all agreed. At daybreak they set sail, running right into the mouth of the storm. The families of the crew all stood on the wharf and cried, fearful for their lives. The only dry eyes belonged to Captain Amos's wife. And when the rest of the families went to church, to pray, Mrs. Amos simply returned to her home, which they shared with her sister and mother.

"The Amos's marriage was reported to be as stormy as the roughest seas, and their arguments were like nothing you've ever heard before."

Guess again, I thought. He'd obviously never lived through a separation.

"And despite the prayers and hopes of the families, the ship didn't return when it was scheduled. Other ships went out once the storm cleared, but the ship and its crew seemed to have just vanished into the dark, deep ocean. There was nothing.

"That is, nothing until the body of Captain Amos was discovered washed up on the shore a few kilometres south. One of the Captain's arms was mangled beyond belief, and one of his legs was gone, ripped off below the knee. At first the rescuers couldn't detect any breath, but finally they became aware of a faint pulse and shallow breathing. They brought him back to the village and laid him in his bed. His wife reacted strangely, as though she hadn't noticed he was gone in the first place or had reappeared, on the verge of death.

"No one had any thought that he could possibly live, but they hoped he could at least tell them what had happened, how the crew had met their end, before he, too, expired.

"Somehow, against all odds, the Captain barely and briefly regained consciousness. He wasn't able to tell them anything. His memory ended when they left port and didn't start again until he was lying in his bed in his house.

"All hope of an answer was abandoned, and the other families were left with nothing but the anguish of knowing that their loved ones had perished — while still clinging to the small shred of hope that if one man could wash ashore, perhaps others could as well. They left Captain Amos to die in the privacy of his home, in the company of his wife.

"But he didn't die. The same stubbornness that drove him in life wouldn't allow him to die. Over the course of the next dozen days he regained his strength, although he never managed to regain his memory of the events that had transpired. And, crippled as he was, he was never able to return to the sea. Stuck at home, he argued endlessly with his wife. Legend has it that the fights became violent at times, but the villagers feared more for him than for her. She was a big woman, outweighing him considerably and standing 6 centimetres taller. As well, of course, she had use of both arms and both legs, and her mother and sister were there to help if needed. All that was left for him was to wander the village and drink.

"Perhaps that's why the Captain agreed to become the keeper — he needed a useful occupation. So he and his wife and his mother-in-law and his wife's sister moved out to the island. They say he even stopped drinking and that he and his wife started to get along. No one knows that for a fact, of course, since they were now seen only by the few people who journeyed to the island for short periods of time. But what the whalers did know was that each night the beam of light shone out from the lighthouse. No more ships were lost, and all seemed well."

"This is where the bad stuff happens," I whispered to Chuckie.

"You call losing a leg and a bunch of people

drowning *good* stuff?" he asked.

"Until that fateful night," Dr. Resney said.

I smiled smugly at Chuckie.

"It was the height of the whaling season. Every single ship in the harbour was out at sea, and aboard those ships was every able-bodied man in the village. They'd been gone for the better part of a week and they were scheduled to return, if not that night then maybe the next or the next. It was a terrible night . . . very much like tonight . . . but the villagers knew that if they came home they would be led by the beacon of the lighthouse. Except that beacon didn't come. Out where there should have been the streak of light was only darkness. They waited, hoping against hope . . . but the light didn't come.

"Word spread from house to house, and the people gathered in the church. There wasn't a single soul in the whole village who didn't have a loved one aboard those ships. If they were to try and come home tonight, not knowing the lighthouse was darkened, ship after ship would be driven onto the rocks. Something had to be done. Somebody had to brave the waves and row out to the island. But who? All the men of the town — and back in those days you were considered a man by the time you were thirteen or fourteen years old — were aboard the ships. The oldest amongst those still in the village were boys of no more than eleven or twelve years of age. Is anybody here eleven or twelve?"

Hands shot up across the room, including mine, and Chuckie's.

"Think about that . . . and remember it was one

hundred years ago, before they realized girls and boys were equal."

"Equal?" Christina's voice called out of the darkness. "Since when are boys as good as girls?"

Laughter and protests drowned out any further comments.

"What would it be like for one of you boys, or girls, to go out in a small rowboat and travel through the high waves, by yourself, in the dark of night, from Roger's Harbor out to this island?"

There was a murmuring of comments from across the room.

"While it was still being decided who would go, one boy turned to his younger brother and told him to wait a few minutes and then tell them that he had already gone. His brother wanted to say something but was warned he'd be 'whipped good' if he told before he was supposed to. The older boy, Ian, slipped out of the hall.

"Ian was twelve years old and in his last year of school . . . sixth form. He would be joining his father and brothers aboard ship the next school year. He moved down to the wharf and quickly put a dory, a rowboat, into the water. He was so young he still felt invincible and didn't fear the waves and the wind. He dipped the oars into the water and pulled away from the wharf. At first the waves were big but not overwhelming. He chuckled to himself, 'Imagine them all being so afraid of waves this small.' He'd ridden far worse.

"Clearing the protection of the harbour, he was hit by the real storm. The driving rain, the wicked wind blowing the whitecaps off waves so high that from the top of one wave to the bottom of the trough was ten metres."

For a few seconds, I tried to place myself along-side Ian in that little boat, but I found the thought so frightening that I retreated back to the safety of my chair in the dining room. I took a sip from my drink.

"Once out there, Ian thought better of what he was doing. He wanted to go back, back to the safety of the harbour, back to the safety of his bed, but he knew he couldn't. By now his brother had told everybody, and to turn back was to be branded a coward. He also thought of all the men on the ships and all their wives and children and elderly parents back in the village. And most of all he thought about his father and three brothers all aboard ship, all in danger. He put his back into the task and rowed harder. Turning back was not an option.

"Ian had been out to the island many a time with his father, for his father was one of the few friends the Captain had. Ian would often sit at their feet and listen to their stories of the sea. On those occasions it had taken almost two hours to row out to the island, but this was far from a normal day. He had already been in the water much longer than two hours.

"The real danger to Ian wasn't just that his boat might be swamped or he'd be washed overboard, but that he might miss the island completely and keep rowing out to sea, farther and farther from the land. With each pull of the oars he wondered, had he missed the island? Just as the last of his hope was draining away he heard something . . . the unmistakable sound of waves crashing against a shore. This sound renewed his strength and he rowed even harder. And as luck would have it he came to shore at exactly the right place, directly in front of the lightkeeper's house. He struggled to pull the boat onto the sandy shore, finally falling down on the beach, exhausted, grateful to be alive and on solid ground, but not knowing if he even had the strength to go on.

"He lay there on the beach for a few minutes. He knew that coming this far without going any farther was no better than staying in the village. He staggered to his feet and started up the uneven path leading from the beach to the house. His mind was filled with questions. What had happened to the Captain and his family? He didn't have to wait long for an answer to part of his question.

"In the dark he tripped over something and fell to the ground. He looked down and his heart was filled with terror as he saw the object over which he'd tripped. It was a body."

A murmur rose from across the room, including a gasp from my own mouth that was a complete surprise until I heard it myself.

"Finally some action," Mike whispered.

"Ian scampered away, still on all fours, terrified. He stopped a few metres away and turned back, hoping the body had somehow vanished, that he'd been mistaken, that it was just an old piece of driftwood the storm had thrown up on the beach. But it was a body . . . there was no mistake. Fighting against the terror gripping his chest he forced himself to rise to his feet and move toward the body. He could see by the long hair and the dress that it was a woman, but he couldn't tell at first who it was. It wasn't just the darkness — the face was bruised and battered and bloodied. He brushed away the hair from her face. It was Mrs. Amos's sister! Looking down from the face he saw that one of her arms, the left one, was mangled and torn. Even worse, one of her legs, the right one, was gone. All that remained was a bloody stump below the knee.

"Now Ian had never seen a dead body before, except for his granny lying in a coffin in the church before her burial. She had seemed so peaceful lying there, just as though she were asleep, except somehow she'd looked finer than usual with her hair all done, wearing her best 'Sunday go to meeting' dress. This body wasn't peaceful or asleep, just dead, and a horrible death it must have been."

Dr. Resney stopped and took another sip from his mug. He then looked at his watch. "I can see it's getting late. Maybe I should stop the story here and I can finish it tomorrow."

A loud chorus of protest erupted around the room. A smile creased his face and he raised his hands to silence us.

"How could this terrible thing have happened? Each and every nerve in Ian's whole body was calling out for him to run back to the dory and row back out to sea. At least he knew the dangers awaiting him there. He took two steps in that direction and then stopped. He thought of his brothers, Vince and Andrew and Samuel, and his father, all out at sea on a whaler, all depending on him. He turned and started for the house. He was being driven by a strength he didn't know he possessed.

"The rain was still driving down hard. Flashes of lightning seared across the sky and lit up the landscape below. The keeper's house became visible for a few seconds with each strike.

"He sprang up onto the wooden porch. The roof provided partial refuge from the rain. He heard a bang and jumped into the air, spinning in the direction of the noise. It was the front door. It was partially open; the wind blew it closed and then it bounced back open again. He moved toward the door and looked down. There was something lying on the floor in the threshold, stopping the door from closing. It was a piece of driftwood. Ian bent down to pick it up. It wasn't until he grasped it firmly in his hand and tried to lift it that he realized it wasn't a piece of wood . . . it was a leg."

There were screams and groans from across the room as Dr. Resney held his arm high in the air, and we could almost see the leg he was holding.

"He dropped it noisily to the wooden floor of the veranda, then backpedalled quickly across the porch, bumping into the railing and almost tumbling over the side.

"Just as he regained his balance, he caught sight of the second body, and he felt his head reel. The body was lying on the porch, face down. While he couldn't see who it was — not without turning the body over — he could see that once again the left arm was mangled and the right leg was missing below the knee. This made three people Ian had seen just like this . . . the two bodies . . . and Captain Amos.

"A noise came from behind Ian and he spun around in time to see a dark shape crawl out of the front door of the house. Ian felt his breath freeze in his lungs and his legs turn to stone. He watched the darkened shape inch forward across the porch. Then it stopped. A flash of lightning split the sky, illuminating the world for a second, and in that second Ian saw the creature . . . it was Mrs. Amos. As the light vanished, the darkened figure slumped to the ground. He rushed to her side and called out her name. She turned her head and looked up at him . . . her eyes were filled with a look of terror that would haunt Ian in his sleep, waking him screaming, for years to come. She reached out her hands and grabbed him by the coat.

"'My husband . . . he's gone crazy,' she gasped, barely able to talk. 'He's got an axe and he's . . . you've got to run . . . get off the island before . . .'

"Her hands slipped from his jacket and she flopped to the floor. He tried to revive her, called out her name again, but it was no use. She was dead.

"Ian's eyes were drawn to Mrs. Amos's body. The left arm was terribly mangled and the right leg was hacked off below the knee."

Dr. Resney took another sip from his mug. The room was completely silent. The hairs on the back of my neck were standing on end. I looked over, first at

Chuckie and then at Mike. Their expressions mirrored my own emotions.

"Just then Ian heard something, or someone, moving around inside the house. It had to be the Captain. Who else could it be? He put one hand on the railing of the porch and leaped over the side onto the sand. He bent down, low to the ground, and tried to gather his wind and his wits. He knew if he were to run there was no way the Captain could catch him. He could sneak into the dunes and get lost in the sand and scrub brush, and the Captain wouldn't even be aware he was there on the island. Or he could run back to the dory and take to the waves. Better to drown than face the same fate as the three women.

"Then another flash of lightning showed him the path he had to follow. The lighthouse was just off to the side and its heavy wooden door was swinging open. He could run for it, go inside and bar the door. He would have to hope the Captain was now too drunk to notice, or too weak to batter through the heavy door.

"There was no decision to make. He sprinted across the sand, his feet barely touching the ground. He didn't dare look back toward the house. He reached the door, grabbed the handle and slammed it shut behind him. In the pitch black, Ian desperately searched with his hands until he found the heavy metal bar to secure the door, and then fumbled with it until it fell into place. He was safe, and he slumped to the ground.

"As his eyes adjusted to the dark, he realized that a thin trickle of light was making its way down the long circular staircase; it was moonlight, coming in through the observatory at the top. He put a hand on the railing and started up the stairs. He'd been to the top before and remembered there were over one hundred stairs. He started counting them in his mind, and some of the stairs answered him back, creaking out a welcome as he climbed.

"When he was halfway up, Ian thought he heard a sound. He stopped and listened. Maybe it was his imagination, or maybe it wasn't. He doubled his pace, taking the steps two at a time. He had to get to the top. Out of breath, Ian turned the last curve of the spiral stairs . . . he was there, within sight of his goal . . . all would be well now.

"'DIE! DIE! DIE!' yelled Captain Amos as he leaped forward at Ian, swinging an axe!"

I jumped slightly out of my seat, hoping nobody had noticed, but I could tell by the screams and gasps that I wasn't the only one who'd reacted.

"Instinctively Ian ducked, and the Captain tumbled over him, falling down the stairs. There was a horrific series of bangs and screams as he rolled and rolled down the stairs until a final *thud* was followed by total and complete silence.

"Ian tried to rise, but his legs were unable to support him. He felt sick to his stomach and feared he would vomit. He curled up into a ball and took deep breaths, trying to force his mind to think about what had to be done instead of what had just happened. Finally, on all fours he crawled over to the base of the light. He racked his brain trying to recall what needed to be done . . . how to feed the oil into the lamp and wind the turntable and set it rotating and light the flame.

"Then he remembered a conversation he'd once overheard between Captain Amos and his father. The entire operation was set and ready each morning. All that would be needed was the striking of a match and the depression of a lever. That was all . . . unless the insanity had overtaken the Captain before the first light of this day.

"Ian found a box of wooden matches sitting on a ledge beside the turntable. He struck one, and the small flame seemed to fill the space. He felt so exposed in the light. As he bent forward, cupping the small flame with one hand, he said a prayer. The light touched the wick and the flame burst to full brightness, reflected and strengthened by the mirrors and lenses that surrounded it. Ian reached out and pushed down on the lever. It started to turn! The light was working! The light was working! The ships would be safe!

"'TURN OUT THE LIGHT! NO ONE SHOULD LOOK AT ME!'

"From far below, the voice filled the tower, and then nothing. Perhaps it was simply the last gasp of the man before he died. Then, Ian could hear the sound — at first quiet, but then unmistakable — of Captain Amos climbing, or really dragging himself, up the stairs.

"The terror that now filled Ian was much greater than all the other fears he had ever felt. He wondered if his heart might simply stop beating from fear. Somehow, this thought seemed almost comforting. Death would rescue him from this fate far worse than dying.

He knew from the sounds he wouldn't have long to wait. The Captain was almost at the top of the stairs.

"The turntable made another revolution and the dazzling light struck Ian, blinding his eyes but giving him a vision of how to survive. He rushed over to the turntable and waited for the beam to strike the top of the stairs. He pulled up the lever, freezing the powerful beam in place. Next he reached over and removed the lid from the container of oil that sat full and ready to replenish the flame. He lifted up the heavy container, careful not to spill any.

"Looking up, he saw Captain Amos standing at the top of the stairs, one hand trying to shield his eyes from the blazing light. The old man's face was swollen and disfigured and Ian hardly recognized him. He was covered with blood — his own, or that of his victims? In his hand was an axe.

"'All must die!' Captain Amos screamed. 'All must die!'

"He took a step to try to move out of the beam and Ian, with all his might, hurled the container of oil. It struck the Captain in the chest, sending him slightly backwards, then splattered up into his face and into his eyes. Captain Amos staggered forward, covered in oil, swinging his axe blindly. Ian scurried across the floor and slid down the opening to the stairs. The Captain lurched forward, flailing about wildly, swearing and cursing at the top of his lungs. Part of his clothing, perhaps the hem of his coat, came in contact with the fire and, soaked in oil, burst into flame. In just seconds the fire spread and the Captain became consumed in flames from head to foot. He raced across the small space, screaming and yelling, before crashing through the glass and falling to the ground below.

"With one final burst of energy, Ian ran over to the turntable and depressed the lever, allowing the light to revolve once more. He moved over to the broken glass and looked down. There, far below, among the sand and rocks, lay the shattered and still burning body of the Captain.

"Ian fell to his knees, exhausted, and stared out into the night. He watched as the beam swept out to sea, and then he realized that the light was being answered! Small jewels danced on the seas. These were the lights of the ships, coming home, and because of him they'd be safe. He closed his eyes and fell asleep.

"And that's how they found him the next morning when they came to the island and pounded on the barred lighthouse door. They soon realized the tale of terror to be told, but of course so much of the story was missing — none of the three dead women, nor Captain Amos, was alive to offer an explanation. In fact, when they searched at the base of the lighthouse, there was not even a trace of Captain Amos's body.

"To this day, people still report sightings of the Captain. Moving around the lighthouse and elsewhere on the island . . . carrying his axe . . . and looking for that boy . . . eleven or twelve years old . . . and seeking his revenge. If you listen in the dead of the night you can sometimes hear him walking through the corridors of this building, softly whispering, '*All must die, all must die.*'"

MONDAY 11:35 P.M.

"That was one spooky story," I said from atop the bunk bed. I kept replaying it over and over in my head.

"Not bad," Mike answered. "Chuckie, will you take the flashlight out of your mouth? You're getting it all slobbery!"

He pulled it out and flashed it in my eyes. "Doesn't it look neat like that, the way it makes the side of my face all glowing and eerie?" Chuckie asked.

There was a knock at the door. We all fell silent. It was long after lights-out and we were supposed to be asleep. A couple of times I'd tried to drift off but I'd been jolted awake by both the noise my two room-mates were making and the fear of what they might do if I fell asleep first.

I heard the door creak open. My mind raced back to the story of Captain Amos, searching for revenge.

"Bed check," came the voice from the dark. It was Ms. Fleming. She walked into the room preceded by the beam of her flashlight.

"There's no use in pretending you're asleep, boys. I could hear you halfway down the hall."

I sat up in bed. Ms. Fleming flashed the light in my face. I shielded my eyes with my hand.

"Gordon, what are you doing in here?" Ms. Fleming asked. "This isn't your room."

"Where else would he be but with us?" Chuckie asked.

She spun the light around to him, illuminating his face, and then turned it to the third bed, where Mike gave her a weak little wave.

"If you three are here, who's in room eight?" she asked.

"Beats me, I wasn't in charge of assigning the rooms," Mike answered.

"Can I assume it's whoever was supposed to be in here?" Ms. Fleming asked.

"You could, I guess," Chuckie said, "but you know what happens when you assume."

"Anyway, we should try to get back to sleep," Mike said, innocently.

"Yeah, right!" she answered. "Now explain to me why you three are in here instead of room eight, where you were assigned . . . in the room directly across from mine."

"Room eight? You said number two," Mike protested.
"No I didn't!"

"We're pretty sure you told us this room, but don't

worry, it doesn't make any difference to us. We're happy here," Chuckie replied.

"Well I'm not happy. Get up and get your things, you're going where you were assigned!"

"Come on, Ms. Fleming, it's the middle of the night. It wouldn't be fair to move us now," Mike argued.

"Not fair? How is it not fair?"

"Well, for starters, it's not fair to the people in the other room. Why should you wake them up because somebody made a mistake . . . not that we're blaming you for the mistake," Chuckie said.

"I didn't make any mistake!" she protested.

"We're not blaming you," Mike said. "But couldn't it wait until tomorrow? What harm can there be in us being in this room tonight?"

There was silence. What he said did make sense. What harm could we do being in here instead of the other room?

"Okay. Fine. The three of you can stay here . . . tonight. Don't cause any trouble . . . and I didn't make any mistake. Good night."

The beam of light receded out the door and she closed it quietly behind her. We all lay silently in our beds. The rain still fell against the window, but it was now just a trickle. I hoped we could finally get to sleep, although I wished I could take Sammy out of the corner of my bag where he was hidden and put him under my head.

"Door or window?" Mike asked.

I rolled over. "What are you two doing?"

"I was asking Chuckie if he figured we should use the door or the window."

"Door, definitely the door. The window doesn't open up wide enough for us to get out," Chuckie answered.

"Out? Why would we want to get out the window?"

"Because there'd be less chance of us being seen than if we have to go out the door," Mike explained.

"But, why are you two going out?" I asked.

"The two of us aren't going out," Chuckie said, and I felt relief. "The *three* of us are going out."

"The three of us? I'm not going anywhere."

"Aren't you at least a little curious about where we're going?" Chuckie asked.

I didn't answer.

"The lighthouse. We're going to the lighthouse."

"You gotta be kidding. Why would you go there?" I asked.

"Looking for a ghost. Captain Amos's ghost," Mike said.

"Are you guys crazy or what?"

"Maybe. Maybe not. But at least we aren't chicken."

"Who's chicken? I just don't want to go out in the middle of the night in the rain," I objected.

"I understand," said Chuckie.

"Yeah, we can't blame him for not wanting to come with us. It would be safer for him to say in bed with his head tucked down under the covers, wearing his little PJs with the sewn-in feet and hoping that the boogie man isn't hiding under the bed," Mike said.

"We should stay put, at least for tonight," I argued,

hoping that by delaying things one night I could stop them completely.

"Nope, tonight is the best night," Chuckie disagreed.

"Yep, best we go tonight. Power's off, teachers are tired, we're in a room as far away as possible from Ms. Fleming. Tonight's the night," Mike said, listing the reasons.

I had to admit he did have logic on his side. He kept on surprising me. For a guy who'd failed once, and supposedly didn't do very well in school, he seemed to be pretty smart.

"Sleep tight, we'll see you later," Chuckie said.

"I'm coming," I interrupted, leaping off the bunk to the ground. "Give me a minute to get into my clothes."

"Make it fast." Mike sounded annoyed that I was coming along, in spite of the way he'd been taunting me.

"I can change as quick as you two can."

"Maybe you can," he countered. "But we've already changed."

Chuckie ran the beam of light up himself and then Mike. They were dressed in clothes, but not what they'd been wearing when we'd headed into the room at the end of the stories. They were both now dressed almost entirely in black.

"But when . . . ?"

"I guess you didn't notice in the dark. When you were getting into your jammies we were getting into our action clothes. Like 'em?" Chuckie asked.

Before I could answer, Mike spoke.

"Wear something black or brown. Nothing white or bright."

"I'll do what I can. Here, let me have the light."

Mike handed it to me. I aimed the flashlight at my suitcase and rummaged around for the most appropriate things I could find. Luckily I'd packed a pair of black sweat pants and a navy blue sweater. I held the two items up for them to see.

"Perfect!" Chuckie congratulated me.

"Yeah, good clothes. Nice teddy bear, too," Mike added.

I slammed the lid down on my suitcase. The beam of light had briefly swept over Sammy while I was searching the bag.

"Ya want him to come along too? You know, in case we need a good snuggle or something?" Mike chided me. He started laughing. "Or if he's a fierce teddy bear, maybe he could protect us from the ghost of Captain Amos."

"Lay off him, Mike," Chuckie interrupted.

"Come on, I'm just razzing him a bit."

"Keep it a bit, unless you want me to start talking about Mr. Buttons," Chuckie said.

"Mr. Buttons?" I asked.

"Yeah, you think you're the only one with a teddy bear? Where is Mr. Buttons, maybe I can talk to him for a minute?" Chuckie asked.

"Shut up or you'll be missing too many teeth to be talking to anybody," Mike answered. He grabbed Chuckie by the front of his shirt. Chuckie didn't look like he was going to back down. I tried to step in between the two of them. They were both half a head taller than me. This was not a good idea.

"Come on guys, I don't know nothing about no teddy bears . . . nobody here has a bear. Right?"

Mike released his grip on Chuckie. "Right. And thanks for pointing that out." Quickly I pulled on my clothes over my PJs and then slipped on my socks and shoes.

"Grab your jackets and let's get going," Mike said.

Chuckie took the lead, and I reluctantly fell in behind him. What was I doing? This was stupid, or worse than stupid. Then I thought about what it would be like to be here for a whole week with no friends. I had no choice.

"Keep moving," Mike ordered as he gave me a not-so-gentle push forward.

I inched into the hall. It was quiet and dark. Mike closed the door to our room. I didn't even hear it kiss against the door frame. Chuckie pushed open the door to the outside, and the sound of the waves against the shore and the smell of the salt air washed in. He slipped out, and I followed. The rain wasn't falling hard but it was still falling. Mike came out last.

"Here," Chuckie said, handing Mike something. "This will wedge the door open."

Mike nodded and took the object, inserting it into the doorjamb. The door remained slightly ajar. Mike moved off away from the building. Within a few seconds he'd disappeared, swallowed up completely by the black of the night. Chuckie tapped me on the shoulder.

"Let's do it, buddy," he said.

We both started moving toward the spot where

Mike had vanished. Within a dozen steps we saw his outline up ahead and moved to his side.

The rain had stopped almost completely. It was more of a light mist now. The ground was sandy and I sank into it as I moved. At least there was no danger of us getting lost. The lighthouse stood out against the night, and I imagined it as the searchlight in a prison yard, hunting for convicts trying to make it over the wall.

We were following a direct line toward the lighthouse. We climbed up the side of a high sand drift. My shoes filled with sand as we surfed down the other side. We scaled the next drift, and the next. Between the drifts were scrub trees, bushes and tall grass.

I started thinking about what would happen if we were caught. We'd be in trouble from the teachers, but I knew my parents wouldn't get too mad at me. Each one would be working so hard to blame the other for my "difficulties," they wouldn't have time to hold me responsible. That was probably the only good thing about this separation thing — no matter what I did wrong it wasn't my fault, it was because of the separation.

"Turn on the flashlight," Mike said to Chuckie.

"Can't do it," Chuckie replied. "It's not working."

"Here, give it to me!" Mike fumbled with it but couldn't produce any light.

"Maybe the rain got to it," Chuckie offered.

"The rain? It's hardly raining at all. More likely you slobbered it up when you kept putting it in your mouth!"

Chuckie shrugged his shoulders. "Sorry. Probably better anyway," he offered. "This way we move completely in the dark. It's not like we won't be able to find the lighthouse."

He was right there. It loomed large on the horizon. What he hadn't mentioned was how we were going to find our way back to school after this was over. The school was dark and low to the ground.

We climbed to the top of a large dune and looked down on the lighthouse. Sitting beside it, just like in the story, was a small house. It looked exactly like I'd imagined it.

"I didn't know there'd be a house," Chuckie said.

"Weren't you listening to the story?" I asked.

"Of course I was, but that was in a long time ago time. I wonder if somebody lives there now."

"Of course somebody does . . . Captain Amos's ghost," Mike said, lowering his voice to a raspy whisper.

"Seriously, if there's a house there must be somebody living there," I noted.

"*Was* somebody living there," Mike replied. "Years and years ago. Remember what Dr. Resney said, it's all controlled from the mainland now."

"This is just the old abandoned lightkeeper's house . . . Captain Amos's house," Chuckie added. "Doesn't it look abandoned?"

In the fragments of light that splintered off from the spotlight I could make out the house. It did look abandoned. The windows were dark, a couple of the shutters hung askew, and the porch railing was missing some spindles. Of course they were right; nobody had probably lived there since long before the three of us were born.

"Let's get going," Chuckie said.

He skidded down the side of the dune. Mike went down after him and I hurried after them. We all bumped together at the bottom.

"What now?" I asked.

"Pictures," Mike answered.

"Pictures?"

"Yes, pictures." He pulled a camera out from under his jacket and held it up so I could see it was one of those instant cameras where the pictures develop in a minute or so. "What's a vacation without pictures? We need some proof to show the guys we were here tonight. Come on and we'll take a few pictures by the lighthouse."

"Cool," Chuckie said. "You never fail to amaze me. Where do you come up with all these ideas?"

"Easy. While the rest of you are wasting your time in class listening to the teacher, I'm thinking. I'll take a picture of you two first."

Chuckie and Mike raced across the open space. I moved more cautiously, keeping one eye on the abandoned house. I had a creepy feeling, like those darkened windows were watching us. I stopped and stared at the house.

"Hurry up if you want to be in the picture," Mike called back to me.

I rushed over and took a spot beside Chuckie against the wall of the lighthouse. "Isn't it too dark for a picture?" I asked.

"You never heard of a flash?" Mike asked. "Say cheese!" he announced, and a flash burst in my eyes. "Now somebody take one of me."

Chuckie took the camera from Mike, and Mike moved beside me. A second picture was taken. Mike was now holding the first picture, which was developing quickly, and Chuckie held both the camera and the second shot. Before our eyes the images started to fill in. At first the figures in the pictures looked ghostlike. That seemed appropriate. As they continued to develop, our features became clearer and clearer until we were unmistakable. Unmistakably goofy looking, that is: red eyes, startled expressions and messy hair. Despite the flash there hadn't been enough light, and the pictures were dark and almost completely colourless.

"You sure you want to show these to the other kids?" I asked.

"How else can we prove we were here at the lighthouse?" Chuckie asked.

"I don't think this will prove anything. This wall could be anything," I replied, pointing to the wall of the lighthouse in the background of the pictures.

"He's right," Mike agreed. "We have to take some other shots. Take one of the lighthouse from a distance and maybe the house . . . yeah, the house, that'll convince them! Come on!"

Mike raced away from the base of the lighthouse. When he was about halfway between the house and lighthouse he stopped. The flash blazed out once, and then twice. He had taken one shot of the house and a second of the top of the lighthouse.

"Here, hold these," Mike said, as he handed me the two shots. "Just handle them around the edge or they'll smear."

"Hey!" Chuckie yelled out.

I practically jumped out of my shoes.

"Take a shot of me here, right where Mrs. Amos's body was found!"

Chuckie was standing in the middle of the porch, right by the front door. He dropped to his knees and then slumped to the floor, trying to imitate the position of Mrs. Amos's body. Mike snapped the shot. In rapid succession he took another of the lighthouse, as seen from the porch, and then two more of the house, blinding me with the second flash practically in my face. He handed two of the pictures to Chuckie and held the last two himself. Mike took a seat on the front step of the porch and we sat on either side of him.

"How are yours turning out?" he asked me.

"Blurry and dark," I answered. One was also a bit crooked but it clearly showed the house, and the second was a bad angle shot of the lighthouse. I showed them the two pictures.

"Let's see yours," Mike said to Chuckie.

"Not bad . . . except what's that?" Chuckie asked, pointing to the corner of one picture.

I looked over and tried to see what he was pointing at. There was a whitish smudge at the top of the picture.

"You smudged it, you jerk! I told you to hold it by the edges," Mike scolded.

"I didn't smudge nothing, and who are you calling a jerk, you jerk!" Chuckie scowled back.

They both got to their feet and the pictures fell like leaves to the floor of the porch. While they were pushing and shoving I scooped the pictures up and looked more closely at the one that had caused the dispute.

There wasn't much light, and my eyes were still sparkling a little from the flash. I held the picture close to my face. The smudge was in the top left corner of the picture and was framed by one pane of the window. The picture was still developing and the details of the house were becoming more distinct by the second. I looked again at the smudge. It was a smudge with eyes and a nose and a mouth . . . and it was wearing a sailor's cap on its head.

I got to my feet. "Guys, you gotta see this!"

They continued to push and shove each other.

"Stop! Both of you stop and look at this picture!" I implored, shoving in between them.

"What? What is it?" Chuckie asked.

"That smudge isn't a smudge."

Mike grabbed the picture and Chuckie struggled to look at it.

"Well, if it isn't a smudge, then what is it?" Mike asked.

As if in answer to his question, the front door of the house opened.

A figure stepped out of the door. I couldn't make out his features as much as I could see his outline. His face was covered with a thick beard and there was a captain's hat atop his head. In one hand he held a long-handled object . . . maybe an axe. I gasped, and felt my heart trying desperately to work its way up my throat. I took a step backwards and stumbled down the steps, landing in the soft, damp sand. Chuckie and Mike looked down at me.

"What are you doing?" Mike demanded angrily.

I reached up and pointed. They both turned toward the house. I expected them to react or jump or something, but they both just froze, as if their brains couldn't comprehend what they were seeing so couldn't issue orders to react to it.

The figure moved out of the shadows. "What do you hooligans want?"

While they didn't have any answers, the question unfroze Chuckie and Mike. They released the grip they still had on each other's jackets and toppled down the stairs, almost landing on top of me.

"What are you doing here?" he yelled.

He came toward us, waving the object he held in his hands. It made a loud, low, swishing sound as it cut through the air. In the darkness I couldn't make out what it was, but it might have been an axe.

"Get offa my property!" he screeched. He brought the object down against the railing with a resounding smash.

Chuckie screamed, and my heart managed to finally push itself right into my mouth. Mike staggered backwards and fell over top of me. I tried desperately to free myself from Mike and started to scurry away on all fours like a crab. Chuckie had already started running. Mike and I bumped heavily together as we both struggled to regain our feet. The weapon smashed against the railing with another resounding smack that cut through the darkness and echoed back at us from the lighthouse. Tripping and bumping together, Mike and I took to our feet and blindly ran after Chuckie. There was a third crash, this time sharper, like the crack of a gun! Was he firing a weapon at us? Was that a rifle instead of an axe he was holding? I needed to move faster. I could imagine the next crack being followed by the searing sting of a bullet piercing my back. Mike was running right beside me. For once I was grateful that he was bigger than me because he made a much larger target.

I tried to speed up but it seemed impossible to move any faster as my feet began sinking into the soft, wet sand. Up ahead Chuckie was barely visible in the darkness, almost at the top of the dune. He'd be safe once he'd dropped over the far side. The sand shifted and swirled under my feet and it felt as if I weren't moving at all, like in one of those nightmares where you're being chased by a monster and your feet are caught in quicksand and the monster is coming closer and closer and closer. I didn't dare look back.

Finally I moved forward. I made the crest of the dune at the same instant as Mike and we both started down the other side. I felt my feet going out from under me and I fell face first into the sand and started rolling down the incline. I bumped to a stop at the bottom.

"Are you okay?" It was Mike. His voice sounded funny, higher pitched and like he wasn't standing beside me. He offered me a hand and pulled me to my feet.

"Thanks," I gasped. My heart was racing and my pulse was so strong I could feel it in my head. "Where's Chuckie?"

"Here . . . I'm here!" He was just behind Mike, sitting in the sand, all balled up with his arms around his curled legs.

"Who was that?" Mike asked.

"It was . . . it was . . . Captain Amos," Chuckie answered.

"Get real," Mike replied. His voice seemed to have almost returned to normal.

"I *am* real. It was a ghost," Chuckie argued.

"It wasn't a ghost. Remember that smudge in the picture? That was the guy we saw," I said.

"So what, then we took a picture of a ghost."

"You can't take a ghost's picture, Chuckie," I reasoned.

"Says who?"

"I don't know . . . that's just what I think from watching television and movies and stuff."

"Gee, thanks for your expert opinion." Chuckie smirked. "I know what I saw, and that wasn't a living being." Even in the thin, dim light, Chuckie looked pale.

"Either way, it doesn't matter. We need to get away from here and back to the school," I argued.

"Right, he's right," Chuckie agreed. "We have to get away from here."

"Which way is back?" I wondered.

"Easy, it's that way," Chuckie answered, pointing to the left.

"No, the other way," Mike objected.

They both looked at me. I shook my head. "I don't know, but what about if we just keep moving that way," I suggested, pointing in the completely opposite direction from the lighthouse. Getting back to the school was important, but not nearly as important as moving farther away from that house.

We started scaling the next sand dune. As I staggered forward I felt something dig into my leg. I reached into my pocket and pulled out three of the Polaroid pictures. They were creased and a bit crumpled. Somehow in the panic and confusion and terror I'd stuffed them into my pocket. Part of me wanted to just drop the pictures to the sand and be done with them. I didn't want any souvenirs from this episode to remind me of what a stupid thing we'd done. How did I ever let these two idiots talk me into this in the first place? It would be better to be friendless than to be going through this. Almost involuntarily, instead of just letting go of the pictures I tucked them into my jacket pocket. That freed up my other hand and I could use both to climb up the dune. Mike and Chuckie had already reached the top and were standing there, peering around as I stopped beside them.

"Let's look around and see if we can get our bearings," Mike suggested.

The dune we stood on seemed to be one of the highest spots around, but the lighthouse was still the only visible landmark. There was a faint outline in the distance that might have been the shore.

"I can't see anything. Let's just keep moving away from the lighthouse. Sooner or later we'll hit the shore and just follow along it."

We skidded down the side of the dune and tried to follow a straight path. The sand was thick and heavy and it was hard to move forward. We crossed a large flat and then started up the dune on the other side.

"What's that?" Mike asked.

"What's what?" said Chuckie.

"Don't you hear something?"

I listened. All I heard was the sea.

"It's getting louder," Mike said. His voice had gotten that strange tone to it again.

"Come on, don't screw around," Chuckie croaked. He sounded genuinely scared.

"I'm not screwing around! Can't you hear it?"

"I can't hear any . . ." Chuckie paused.

I figured he'd just heard what I had. It was a sort of beating sound. I couldn't describe it, but in my mind I pictured something moving across the dunes . . . chasing after us.

"Come on, let's get going!" I practically yelled.

We scrambled up the dune, our hands and feet digging into the shifting sands, racing to reach the top. The sound was getting louder and louder. I looked over my shoulder and the entire sky seemed to have erupted into light. A blazing beam was charging straight toward us, as if the lighthouse itself had come off its base and was chasing us.

"Look out!" I screamed.

The searing light illuminated Chuckie's face beside me and I saw the terror I felt reflected in his eyes. I stumbled down the other side of the dune, just barely aware of Chuckie and Mike falling with me. The noise was overwhelming and the light blinding, and then it swooped past and was gone. The noise receded into the distance. I tried to wipe away the sand that was stinging my eyes and spat it out of my mouth.

"A helicopter," Chuckie said, saying what we all knew.

"What's a helicopter doing out here?" Mike asked.

"I just hope it isn't . . ." I let the sentence trail off.

"You hope it isn't what?" said Mike.

"I hope it hasn't been sent to look for us."

"Oh my God. If they found us missing and called out the police or the coast guard, then we're in major trouble," Chuckie said anxiously.

Uneasily I got back to my feet. I started back up the dune we'd just tumbled part way down. Reaching the top I scanned the horizon. The bright lights of the helicopter were visible. It seemed to be hovering in one spot, or maybe it had set down. At least if nothing else we now had a beacon to guide us to the school.

"It's that way," I shouted, pointing out the direction. "We'd better hurry." The longer we were away the bigger the trouble. "It doesn't look very far."

We redoubled our efforts. Our path seemed to run in a valley between two high drifts and we were able to move quickly. We climbed a small rise and found ourselves overlooking the school and the helicopter. I could see a few people moving in the light.

I turned to Mike and Chuckie. "Let's get it over with." They both nodded solemnly.

Again I felt like a prisoner in a movie, except this time I was walking the last mile on my way to the gas chamber — and there was no chance of a last-minute call from the governor to save me. We were dead, or even worse than dead — waiting to be dead.

The blades of the chopper were still spinning but at a much slower speed. Getting closer I could feel the breeze they made. I shaded my eyes against the bright lights and I could make out figures but couldn't see who was there. It really didn't matter. We needed to just go and turn ourselves in and try to explain everything . . . for all the good that would do. I wondered which of my parents would have to come up and get me when they kicked the three of us out.

Mike grabbed me by the arm and guided me around the side of the helicopter. I nodded and followed willingly. We curved along and came back toward the figures from the side of the helicopter closest to the school.

Chuckie leaned over and put his mouth close to my ear so I could hear him over the sound of the chopper. "You think there's any way we can talk our way out of this?"

I shook my head.

"Me neither," he admitted.

Chuckie took the lead and we walked toward the closest figure. As we got closer it became obvious that it was a man. He wore some sort of flight jacket and I assumed he was the helicopter pilot. Ms. Fleming came out of the school. She saw us at the same instant I saw her. Her eyes glared even brighter than the searchlights of the helicopter. I swallowed hard as she started toward us.

"Ms. Fleming —" I started to say.

"Inside!" she yelled over the din of the helicopter, pointing toward the school. She turned back and we hurried after her. Mike ran up ahead in time to open the door for her. We followed her to the dining room, which was dark and deserted.

"What do you three think you're doing? I told everybody to go back to bed!"

"But . . . but . . ." I stammered.

"I don't want any buts!"

"Coming through!" called out a voice from behind.

I spun around. Two men were rushing up the corridor pushing a stretcher. Dr. Resney's wife was on it. They rushed by us and one of them kicked open the door. They collapsed the legs of the stretcher as they squeezed through the doorway. With one at each end, they carried it off toward the waiting helicopter.

"Wait for me!" Dr. Resney yelled out. He brushed by us carrying a suitcase and ran out the door after them.

"What's happening?" Chuckie asked.

"What do you mean? I've already explained it to everybody . . ." Ms. Fleming stopped and got a confused look on her face. "You three really don't know, do you?"

I shook my head.

"You mean you three were in bed when I explained everything . . . I'm so sorry . . . I shouldn't have raised my voice . . . it's just, everything has gone so wrong . . . and then all the kids got up and I had to send everybody back to bed . . . I should have realized you three weren't even there . . . you were almost the only ones who were asleep . . ."

"We weren't asleep, we were . . ."

"Awake but stayed in the room," Mike interrupted.

What was he talking about? What was going on here?

"And it's okay, Ms. Fleming, honestly," Chuckie said.

"Yeah, no sweat," Mike chipped in. He shot me a dirty look. "But could you tell us what's happening?"

All at once the noise of the helicopter filled the room. Ms. Fleming moved toward the window and motioned for us to follow. We reached the glass in time to see the chopper start to lift off. The noise grew even louder as it gained elevation. The bright searchlights were turned off, leaving just the little red and white running lights shining. The chopper veered and spun around and then shot off, vanishing over one of the high dunes. The room was suddenly silent.

"That was a medivac helicopter. Mrs. Resney went into labour and they had to get her to the hospital," Ms. Fleming said, breaking the quiet.

"But by helicopter?" I asked.

"It was an emergency. Besides, there aren't any ships available. Dr. Resney was monitoring the radio and he told me the storm hit the mainland very hard. Boats have been tossed onto the land, roofs torn off houses, massive flooding, and they evacuated people from the coast."

"Wow, some storm!"

"But what happens to us?" I asked.

"He said they'd send back a couple of substitutes to run the program, but they probably won't get here until late tomorrow."

"And until then?" I asked anxiously.

"Until then, Mrs. Murphy, and myself, and of course Mrs. Presley will look after things. But first things first. I want you three to get to back to bed."

3:01 A.M.

I was so tired I figured I'd fall asleep the minute my head hit the pillow, but instead I kept playing the night's events over in my head. I tried to snuggle down into the pillow. At best I might get a few hours of sleep before breakfast.

I perked up my ears; somebody was moving around the room. Chuckie or Mike probably had to go to the bathroom. My thoughts were confirmed when I heard the water running. I tried to sink down lower into the mattress but came back to life when I heard whispering. Why would there be whispering . . . and giggling? I held my breath and tried to open my ears wider.

"Is he asleep?" Chuckie whispered.

There was a pause, but out of the slits of my eyes I could see a darker darkness peek over the edge of my bunk and then clunk down on the floor.

"He's asleep . . . pass me the bowl."

Those goofs were going to try to get me! I wanted to jump up and yell at them and throw the water in their face and . . . but they'd just try it again another night. There was another way.

I relaxed and let my arms lie limp at my sides. I took a deep breath and let the air whistle a little bit as it came back out through my nose. Somebody touched my hand. I had to fight the urge to jump. My arm was pulled up and something, a pillow, was placed underneath it to prop it in place. My hand hung down. There was more whispering and giggling

ERIC WALTERS

and then I felt my hand being dipped into warm water. It was almost comforting, and I felt a little tingling inside. I could see how this could make things happen . . . if you were asleep. I stayed motionless, although I couldn't help but smile — a smile I knew they couldn't see in the dark. I knew the two of them were standing down there, waiting. It felt good to keep them waiting.

"Is it happening?" Chuckie whispered.

I couldn't make out the words in his response but he definitely sounded disappointed. They whispered back and forth to each other and then I felt my arm being lifted up once again and my hand slipped out of the bowl of water. Now I could get to sleep.

TUESDAY 7:45 A.M.

I opened my eyes. It was light. Morning. My mind instantly jumped into the events of last night. None of it seemed real . . . it was like a dream . . . but it wasn't. I stretched and yawned. That was the longest night I could ever remember, but it was over, and somehow I'd survived it unscathed.

I sat up, threw my legs over the side and jumped down. Chuckie was sitting on the edge of the bottom bunk. Mike rolled over and sat up.

"That was some night!" Chuckie exclaimed.

"It seemed more like a week. I can't believe how much happened yesterday," I replied.

The two of them looked at each other and started to giggle.

"What's so funny?" I asked.

"Oh, nothing . . . nothing at all," Chuckie answered, and he poked Mike in the ribs with his elbow.

"I'm hungry. Let's go down for breakfast," I suggested.

"Yeah, I'm hungry too, and thirsty," Mike replied.

He bent down and pulled his suitcase out from under the bed. He clicked the latches and the lid popped up. Then he reached in and brought out a six-pack of Coke. He pulled one free, ripped off the tab and tipped it back to his mouth. His Adam's apple bobbed up and down as he chugged it. Mike lowered the can and then crushed it, tossing it toward the garbage can on the far side of the room. It clanked off the wall, hit the edge of the garbage can and settled into the bottom.

"Two points!" he exclaimed.

I shook my head. "You drink Coke for breakfast?" I asked in amazement.

"Coke is nature's perfect breakfast drink," Mike said, smiling. "You think something's wrong with that?"

"Everybody thinks there's something wrong with that," Chuckie interjected. "But you don't even know the worst," he continued, speaking to me. "I've seen him pour it on his cereal."

I felt myself shudder.

"Hey, I only did that once . . . or twice. Usually I just drink it. One a day, like the vitamins."

"I think I'll stick to my Flintstones if you don't mind," I chuckled.

"You'd better stick to them," Mike said threateningly. "These are the only Cokes on the whole island."

"How do you know that?"

"Believe me, I know," he answered. "I have five more Cokes for five more mornings. None for anybody else, understand?"

"Don't look at me!" Chuckie replied. "I'm a Pepsi man myself. Besides, I know how grumpy you get without your Coke."

What an awful thought: Mike being grumpier than he already was.

"I won't touch them either," I assured him.

"Good! Now that we all agree on that, let's get dressed and go for breakfast."

"And don't forget to shave," Chuckie added.

"Shave? Do you shave?" I asked.

"Not me," Mike admitted. "Except my head."

"Me neither," Chuckie added.

"Well who do you think should shave . . . ?" I let the sentence trail off as the two of them laughed out loud.

I rushed to the washroom, looked into the mirror and took two steps backwards. A thick black moustache with twirly ends was painted onto my upper lip. I reached up and touched it; it was solidly in place. I turned on the tap, and while the water was running I grabbed a facecloth and soap and lathered it up. I rubbed the cloth against my face hard and then rinsed the suds away with fresh water. When I looked up at my reflection in the mirror, I was shocked to see the image hadn't faded a bit.

I redoubled my effort, scrubbing it so hard my skin hurt. I used the edge of my fingernail to try to scrape some of it away. Again I rinsed off all the lather. The moustache was still completely intact, and it looked even blacker now in contrast to the redness of my skin, which had been irritated by the scrubbing. I caught sight of their reflections in the mirror, peering into the bathroom, stupid grins on their faces. I spun around.

"What's the idea!" I demanded. My hands curled into fists.

"Don't look at us. Maybe it was the moustache fairy," Mike suggested, and Chuckie started giggling again.

I wanted to take my fist and swipe the grins off both their faces, but I knew that, most likely, I'd just end up with a bleeding nose or a fat lip to go with the moustache. This wasn't funny, not funny at all!

"It makes you look older. I heard some of the girls talking about you and somebody . . . I didn't hear who they were babbling about, but maybe your girlfriend will be impressed with your new moustache," Chuckie added.

"She won't be impressed . . . I mean, I don't have a girlfriend! We were just talking!"

"Ah, obviously a story here. Want to tell us about it?" Chuckie teased.

"No! What I want is to know how to get this thing off, now!" I was struck by the fear that they'd used some sort of permanent marker and it would take days or even weeks to fade away.

"Don't worry, we'll tell you how to get it off . . . eventually," Mike chuckled.

"Eventually? I need to know now! I can't go down to breakfast like this! What will all the kids say?"

"Not to mention your girlfriend," Chuckie chipped in.

"I don't have a girlfriend," I protested. "And what will Mrs. Murphy and Ms. Fleming say?"

Chuckie and Mike exchanged looks. "He's got a point there."

"Yeah, I do." There was more than one way to skin a cat. I pushed between them in the door frame and turned toward the door to the hall. "I'm going down for breakfast now. I'm not even going to change."

"You can't!" Chuckie exclaimed, rushing past me to block the door.

"Why can't I?"

"You gotta get that moustache off first or we'll get in trouble!"

"I will get it off . . . eventually."

"Eventually? You gotta do it now, before the teachers see it!" Chuckie exclaimed.

"But if I take it off now my girlfriend won't see it. Didn't you guys say it made me look older?"

Mike tapped me on the shoulder. I turned around.

"Here, this'll take it off," he said. He handed me a plastic bottle. I looked at the label; it was rubbing alcohol. I worked hard not to smile, but I couldn't completely hide my smirk.

"And this will work?" I asked, not willing to believe anything he said at this point.

"Yeah, that'll take it off," Chuckie said, answering for Mike. "Honest. We play jokes on friends, but we don't lie to them."

"Friends?"

"Of course . . . what else would we be?" Chuckie asked.

I took the bottle and retreated into the bathroom.

8:25 A.M.

By the time we'd washed and dressed, not to mention "shaved," we were among the last kids in the dining room.

"Let's sit over there," Chuckie said. He pointed to a table occupied by Christina and her two roommates, Jenna and Lauren. There were three vacant seats.

"With my sister again? Wasn't last night enough? I don't even like sitting with her when I'm at home!" Mike protested.

"Come on, it's been days since I've bugged her. I bet you I can get her all annoyed before she finishes breakfast," Chuckie replied.

"No bet. Just sitting there will get her all annoyed, even if you don't do anything," Mike countered.

Chuckie walked over to the table and the two of us trailed after him.

"Mind if we join you ladies?" he asked.

"No, that would be fine," Jenna replied cheerfully.

"It would?" Chuckie couldn't believe his ears.

"Sure, come and sit down. Here, you can have my seat, Gord, and I'll move over," Lauren offered.

"That's okay, don't go to any trouble."

"No trouble at all," she giggled. She got up and moved to the other side of Jenna, leaving a vacant seat beside Christina.

Reluctantly I sat down. Mike followed suit. Chuckie seemed so stunned by the girls voluntarily allowing us to sit down that he remained standing. Finally Mike grabbed him by the arm and pulled him into the last vacant seat.

"Is cereal all there is to eat?" Mike asked.

"Yep, and bread with jam or butter. Nothing hot, not even toast, until they fix the generator."

"I guess that'll have to do," Mike lamented. He rose to his feet.

"Sit down," Christina ordered. "Each table has two runners who have to get breakfast for the rest of the table."

"You mean like waiters?" he asked.

"Or waitresses," Jenna added.

"Whatever. Who are the runners?" Chuckie asked.

"It changes every day. For the first meal it's the youngest person in each group of three who has to serve the other two."

"That leaves me out," Mike said proudly.

Chuckie looked at me. "My birthday is April 23rd. When's yours?"

"September 19th. I guess that makes me the youngest," I said.

I stood up reluctantly and they gave me their orders. I headed off to the buffet table and took a tray to carry the food. I turned around and Christina was right behind me.

"I'm the youngest, and the girls wanted more cereal," she explained. She furrowed her brow and stared like she was studying me. "What happened to your face?"

"What do you mean?"

"It looks all red and irritated, especially over your lip . . ." She chuckled. "They drew something on your face when you were sleeping, didn't they?"

I nodded. "A moustache."

"I knew sharing a room with them would be an adventure for you."

"You have no idea what an adventure."

"What do you mean?"

I looked around in both directions. Nobody was close enough to hear.

"Here, look at this," I said, pulling one of the pictures out of my pocket. I figured it was all right to show her because Mike was planning on showing them to other people anyway.

She held it up. "What is this?"

"The lighthouse."

"What lighthouse?" she asked.

"The one here on the other side of the island."

"But how did you get a picture of the lighthouse?" she asked, her voice rising noticeably.

A couple of heads turned. "Shhhh!" I took the picture back and stuffed it in my pocket. "We took it last night . . . we were there."

"Are you three crazy? Forget that question — I already know about the other two. Are you crazy too?"

"I don't know. They just started talking and then Mike said something and then something else and before I knew it I was standing at the base of the lighthouse."

"That sounds like Mike. He can convince anybody

to do anything," Christina admitted. "I don't even want to think about the things he's talked me into doing over the years. And he never seems to run out of new ways to get into trouble."

"Yeah, he does seem very creative," I agreed. "But how can he be so smart about things like that and be so . . ." I let the sentence trail off, thinking better of it.

"And be so stupid at school?" Christina asked, finishing my thought and sentence.

Reluctantly I nodded in agreement.

"That's just Mike. He's got some learning problems. He's smart but he can't put things down on paper very well. He's really about the smartest person I know, but don't tell him that I told you that, okay? He doesn't like people talking about it."

"Which part, the learning problems or being really smart?"

"Both."

"I won't mention it," I promised.

I finished loading up the tray and brought it back to the table. Mike and Chuckie dug in like they hadn't eaten for weeks. I looked up and saw Jenna and Lauren looking at me, smiling. They both giggled and looked back down at their fresh bowls of cereal. Why were they looking at me that way?

"You two are crazy!" Christina declared loudly.

Chuckie looked at her with a puzzled look on his face. "Well, yeah, but do you have a point?"

"Yeah, I have a point! What were you doing sneaking out last night?"

"Christina!" I exclaimed in shock.

"You guys snuck out?" Lauren asked.

Chuckie broke into a huge smile. "Wanna see the pictures?"

"Pictures! You took pictures?" Jenna asked.

"Yeah, they took pictures," Christina said, shaking her head sadly. "Not only are they stupid, but they figured we needed proof that they're stupid. Show 'em the pictures, Gord."

"You already showed them to my sister?" Mike asked. "Now that was bright."

"But you were going to show them to people anyway, weren't you?"

"People yes, my sister no. But it's too late now. Show them the pictures."

I rose slightly out of my seat to dig the pictures back out of my pocket. I handed them to Christina.

"I didn't know you took more than one shot," Christina said.

"We took six or seven," Mike replied.

"But there are only three here," Christina said. She passed the first one to Jenna.

"We lost the others when the ghost surprised us," Chuckie said.

"Ghost, what ghost?"

"No ghost," Mike answered. "There was no ghost."

"There was a ghost! We even took a picture of it!" Chuckie argued.

"Where? I'd like to see that picture," Jenna exclaimed.

"That's one of the ones that got lost," Chuckie replied.

"It wasn't a ghost. It was just some guy at the lighthouse," Mike argued.

"There was somebody at the lighthouse?" Christina asked in amazement.

"Yeah, there's a house beside it and he must live there or something," Mike explained.

"Not a person . . . a ghost," Chuckie insisted.

"I can prove it's just a person . . . tonight," Mike said slyly.

"Tonight?" three of us said in unison.

"Yeah, tonight . . . when we go back."

"You are worse than crazy, Mike!" Christina exclaimed. "Stop pushing your luck. If you get caught and sent home Dad'll kill you."

"He might," Mike admitted. "But he will kill me for sure if I don't bring back his new camera."

"What do you mean?"

"I dropped it when we were startled by that guy. It fell right beside the steps. I figure I can go and get it later on."

"But won't it be ruined anyway, being left outside all night?" Jenna asked.

"It's waterproof. It'll be okay . . . I hope," Mike replied. "I guess I'll know for sure tonight."

"Can we come along?" Lauren asked.

"No, we can't come along, because they're not going!" Christina exclaimed.

"Not going where?" Ms. Fleming asked. We were all so preoccupied with the discussion that nobody had noticed her coming up to our table.

"To get more food," Christina said.

"Good morning, Ms. Fleming," Mike sang out sweetly. "I hope you're still not feeling bad about last night."

She looked slightly embarrassed.

"Have you heard anything about the Resneys?" Jenna asked.

"Nothing, and we won't be hearing anything," she replied.

"I don't understand."

"Mrs. Presley told me the batteries on the radio are dead. She figures Dr. Resney was so excited last night that he forgot to turn the radio off after he called for the helicopter."

"So we have no electricity, no instructors, no radio and no idea about when somebody might be here."

"Yeah, that pretty much sums it up, Gordon. What are the pictures?" Ms. Fleming asked.

"Pictures? Oh these are nothing," Christina answered. She took the two she had in her hands and stuffed them in her pocket. I did the same with the one I was holding.

"They're obviously something," Ms. Fleming said suspiciously.

"They're just . . . just . . . um . . ." I stammered.

"Gordon and I were exchanging school pictures," Christina jumped in.

My jaw dropped so far I was afraid it would clunk against the table. Jenna and Lauren started to giggle again.

"The three of us should sit down and talk," Ms. Fleming announced very seriously.

"A talk? Do we really need to talk?" I asked.

"We do, but not right now. Later, just the three of us. But first things first. We should all finish up breakfast and head down to the beach for some exploring.

9:25 A.M.

Stepping outside, it was like the storm had never happened. The sky was clear and the sun was bright and warm. The air smelled good — fresh, and with the strong scent of the ocean. We were among the last few kids out and we trooped over to Ms. Fleming, who was standing beside a storage shed.

"Here, take this," she said, handing me a long-handled net.

"Nice net, Gordo!" Chuckie chuckled.

I did feel sort of strange holding onto the net, I had to admit, at least to myself.

"Glad you like it, Chuckie, because here's an identical one just for you," Ms. Fleming told him.

Everybody in the class was carrying some sort of scoop or bucket or net. She led us to the water.

The storm was gone but its effects remained on the shore. Pieces of driftwood, long strands of seaweed and dead fish littered the beach. For the first time I felt caught up in the excitement of the trip. There was no telling what we might find here.

As I trailed along behind everybody, poking and prodding and checking out the debris on the sand, I realized that I hadn't even been thinking about my mother and father and the separation — not at all. My mind had been free of all that garbage for at least a little while. It felt good to know that I could forget about it, even if it was only for a few hours.

"Excellent!" Ms. Fleming pronounced excitedly. "Plenty of samples for us to collect. Let's spread out and see what we can find. Oh, and everybody please be careful of jellyfish."

"What's a jellyfish?" Chuckie asked.

"It's not really a fish. It's a type of invertebrate. It looks a lot like a plastic bag filled with water."

"You mean like this?" Chuckie asked, bending down.

"Don't touch it!" Ms. Fleming screamed.

Chuckie jumped back and she hurried over.

"Even if it's dead it can still give a painful sting," she explained. "Everybody look at this. If you find one, just leave it."

We spread out across the tidal flat. Along with all the things that had been blown or thrown up onto the beach, the flats were dotted with pools of water. I bent down to look in one of the larger pools. I caught sight of movement and a little minnow flitted across the pool. A bright orange crab moved after it.

"Uggg!" I shouted in disgust as a smelly, slimy net was lowered over my head. I struggled and pushed it off.

"Heck, I had a big one, but it got away!" Chuckie screamed.

"GUYS!"

I turned away from Chuckie to the voice. It was Mike, waving to us from farther down the beach.

"I wonder what he found?" Chuckie asked.

"Probably a ghost," I answered. "But why don't we go and check?"

We trotted along the sand. "What is it?"

"Nothing, and I figure we won't find nothing exciting if we keep looking in the same places as everybody else," Mike replied. "Let's head down the beach where nobody's been yet."

We started to walk away. I looked back over my shoulder and saw Christina coming up the beach after us. I was glad she was coming in our direction.

"What's she doing?" Mike asked pointedly. "Probably going to spy on me so I don't do anything wrong. She keeps forgetting I'm the older one. Come on, let's lose her!"

He started running, followed by Chuckie, and reluctantly I ran after them. We rounded a point of land and Christina, and everybody else, was lost from view.

"That'll give her something to worry about," Mike panted.

"What's that?" Chuckie asked.

"Where?" I questioned.

"Up there, along the beach."

"I can't see anything," Mike said.

"Way up ahead," Chuckie directed. "It looks like the storm threw up a bunch of logs onto the beach."

Christina came running around the point. She stopped running when she saw us and slowed to a walk. It was an angry walk. I turned back to look in the direction Chuckie had been pointing.

"Let's get a closer look," I suggested. Something

about those "logs" didn't look like logs.

"Let's go," Mike responded. "And quick."

Christina yelled something after us, but she was too far away for me to make out the words. You could tell she was angry, though. We hurried up the beach. My eyes were riveted ahead while the two others seemed more concerned about the charging Christina. Finally she caught up and grabbed Mike by the arm, and he and Chuckie stopped. I kept moving.

"You can't go to the lighthouse. You have to come back right now or I'm going to get Ms. Fleming!" she threatened.

"You better go and do that," I said over my shoulder.

"You *want* me to get Ms. Fleming?"

"Yeah, go and get her."

"Why?" Mike asked.

"She'd better see this," I answered. "Those aren't logs . . . they're alive."

"Alive . . . give me a break," Chuckie snickered. "You'll have to do better than that if you want to try and fool me."

"I'm not trying to fool anybody," I argued. "I saw one move, I really did!"

"Yeah, right . . ." Chuckie started to say before he was interrupted by Christina.

"He's not kidding, Chuckie, I just saw it too . . . at least I think I did. Close your mouth and open your eyes!"

We all stared in silence for a few seconds.

"Does anybody have any idea what they are?" I asked.

"No idea," Mike said. "But let's go close enough to find out."

Christina looked anxious. "Do you think we should?"

"We? I don't think *we* should do anything. I think Chuckie and Gord and me should go closer and *you* should go away."

"You're not going anywhere without me!" she protested.

We started down the beach and I started counting. Whatever they were, there were seven of them scattered across the flats and in the shallow waters. Some of them were much larger than the others. Then my attention was caught by something breaking the surface of the water just offshore. It was a dorsal fin. It disappeared beneath the water again.

I wasn't the only one who'd seen the fin break the surface. "Wow! There are gigantic fish out there!" Chuckie exclaimed.

"Not fish." My heart was pounding and it wasn't simply from our run along the beach. "That was a whale . . . just like those, on the beach."

"Come on, get real," Chuckie began. "Why would a bunch of whales be up on the beach?"

"They're stranded," Mike explained.

"What do you mean stranded?" I asked.

"They get beached on land. Something happens to them and they end up being left when the tide goes out. It happens all the time. Especially to pilot whales."

"How do you know that?" Chuckie asked in amazement.

"I saw a show on TV. It was about a pod of them stranding on a beach," he explained.

"Like this?" I asked.

"Exactly like this, except there were more of them.

I think over two hundred whales."

"So . . . those aren't logs . . . those are . . . whales," Chuckie said solemnly.

Mike turned slowly to Christina. "Go and get Ms. Fleming, right now."

"But —"

"Don't give me any argument. Go right now!" His tone of voice left no mistake about who was in charge. Without saying another word she ran off.

"I'll come with you," Chuckie offered. He dropped his net and they ran off.

"And Chuckie, Christina!" Mike yelled. They turned around. "Just tell Ms. Fleming. We can't have everybody trooping around them. Okay? She should come with as few kids as possible!"

They nodded in agreement and started off again.

"Come on," Mike commanded, and I instantly followed behind him as he started toward the whales. We walked slowly forward.

My eyes were fixed on the first whale. It was dark in colour, totally black along its back, fading to grey along the sides. There was nothing to really judge it against, but it looked to be three or four metres long. A long fin protruded out the side and rested on the sand. We stopped a few paces away. I felt awed by the sight of this massive whale.

"Wow," Mike said.

"Wow is right." It just didn't seem that it could be real. It was like it was some sort of museum display, made of plaster and plastic, that had somehow had been left on the beach.

"Do you think it's still . . . still alive?" I asked.

"I don't think so. It isn't moving, or even breathing."

Mike moved in closer. I hesitated, but then followed, keeping my distance as he circled around to the front. Maybe it was dead, but it was a lot bigger than me, and I wasn't getting any closer than I had to.

Mike didn't hesitate at all; he moved in and stood right by its side. It had a big, rounded head, a large mouth curving upwards and two little eyes. The eyes were closed and the mouth was almost one metre across.

"I'd hate to be bitten by this," I commented, leaning in as close as I dared.

"Never happen. Whales, even killer whales, never ever hurt or attack people. This type eats squid and fish."

"You know a lot about them."

"I know lots of things. Animals are interesting — a lot more interesting than people. Whoa!" Mike yelled, stepping backwards suddenly.

"What? What?" I asked anxiously, and I too bounded backwards a few steps.

"Its eye!" he said, pointing to the whale. "It moved its eye!"

"Are you sure?"

"Yeah, I'm sure and —"

His sentence was cut off by the sound of escaping air. The whale's whole body sank and then rose as it filled its lungs with air. The whale was taking a breath.

"It's still alive," I said in amazement. It was shocking enough to be standing beside a dead whale, and not believable at all to be so close to one that was alive.

"Yeah, but not very alive, and probably not for long."

I saw movement and looked up and away from the whale. Ms. Fleming, along with Chuckie, Christina and maybe a dozen other kids, was coming across the beach toward us. They were moving quickly.

"They've got to be quiet," Mike ordered. "When whales are like this, they get distressed by noise."

"I'll tell everybody."

I ran along the beach to intercept them. The sand was hard and practically flat. I saw the look on Ms. Fleming's face. It was a combination of shock and amazement.

"Mike says everybody has to be quiet or it'll hurt the whales," I announced as they gathered around me.

"This is unbelievable," she said softly. "Unbelievable. They're still alive?" It sounded more like a statement than a question.

"At least the first one is. We haven't checked out the others yet. It isn't wise for us to stand too close, either." Of course Mike hadn't said anything like that, but I didn't want them to be right beside the whale, leaving me standing in the back looking like a coward.

In silence they followed behind me. Reaching the first whale, everybody fanned out until they formed a circle around it. I looked around at the assembled kids. Their faces showed a mixture of wonder, amazement and total disbelief. Every eye but mine was on Mike, who was crouched over, just away from the head of the creature.

"Are you sure it's alive?" Christina asked.

Mike nodded his head solemnly.

"Look at them all!" Jenna said, astonished. "How many are there?"

"I counted seven on the beach and in the shallow water, but I've seen a couple of fins in the water. There must be more out there."

"Look!" Christina called, pointing out to the bay.

We all turned to look. Not too far offshore a large, dark figure was sticking out of the water. As we looked it disappeared beneath the waves.

"What was that?" Jenna asked in alarm.

"That was a whale spy-hopping," Ms. Fleming responded.

"Spy-hopping?" two kids asked in unison.

"Yeah, they do that to look around. They were checking us out," Mike observed.

"What could have happened to these whales?" Chuckie asked. "Why are they on the beach?"

"It could be a lot of things," Ms. Fleming started to answer.

"Scientists don't know for sure. They think maybe it has something to do with parasites or sickness in the leader, or maybe they get confused by electro-magnetic fields," Mike answered.

"That's impressive, Mike," Ms. Fleming replied.

"I know some things," he answered, not taking his eyes off the whale.

"Yeah, but how did they get so high up on the beach?" Chuckie asked.

"Maybe they got driven up this high by the storm,

and now the tide is going out, stranding them," Ms. Fleming responded.

"Maybe they're just resting," one of the girls suggested.

"Resting?" Mike asked.

"You know, maybe they were tired because of the storm and they needed to come up on the beach for a while until they're feeling stronger. When I was at Sea World the trainer had the killer whales come on the deck to get fish," she continued.

"Are you cra—" Mike started to answer, but Ms. Fleming cut him off abruptly.

"It would be nice if that were the case, but I'm afraid it isn't. Something happened . . . something bad," she said as she reached out and placed a hand on the girl's shoulder.

Mike turned away. "Let's look at the others." He stood up and started toward the other whales. Without word or question, everybody, including Ms. Fleming, followed after him. It seemed pretty obvious to me who was in charge right then.

The next three whales were closely grouped together. Two were large, although not as big as the first, and the third was much smaller. I couldn't help but think they looked like a family — a mother, father and a baby. One of the whales inhaled noisily and Christina screamed in surprise. Mike shot her a dirty look. All three of these whales had their eyes open. They were large, moist, sad-looking eyes. The little one looked scared. Mike reached over and touched the side of one of them.

"Mike, should you be doing that?" Ms. Fleming asked.

"I had to see if it was getting dry."

She nodded. "And?"

"Felt kind of dry."

The remaining three whales were languishing in shallow water, only barely covered. All of them, except for one, which was the largest and farthest out of the water, were "aimed" with their noses pointing to the land and their tails toward the ocean. The big one was lying parallel to the water's edge.

"At least some of them are still in the water," Lauren observed. That was the first word anybody had said in a while. It was like we were all in some sort of supernatural trance, unable to process or believe what our eyes were seeing.

"For now. The tide is still going out. Those three whales in the shallows will be left high and dry long before low tide," Ms. Fleming said.

"When does that happen?" Chuckie asked.

"High tide was just after nine o'clock this morning. The water will keep going out until about three-fifteen," she answered.

"And how long before the water gets back up here to where the whales are?" I asked.

"The next high tide isn't until nine-thirty tonight."

"But can they survive that long out of water?" There was a catch in my voice.

Ms. Fleming looked away and didn't answer.

Mike got up and wiped the sand off his hands. "They can't."

"They can't? How do you know?" Christina asked.

"I just know. They can't stand to be out of water that long. They get badly sunburned and dry out. Even if they get back into the water they still just die."

The expressions of wonder faded from people's faces as it dawned on each of us that we were witnessing the slow death of these animals.

"We should go back and join the rest of the children and Mrs. Murphy," Ms. Fleming suggested.

"Go back?" Mike asked in amazement. "You mean just leave them?"

She nodded her head. "There's nothing we can do. Perhaps the radio is working now, or Dr. Resney has returned, or . . ." Her sentence trailed off. She knew, and everybody else knew, that none of those things was going to happen. She was just trying to get us away so we wouldn't be standing there, helpless, watching the life drain out of the animals.

"They're going to die, aren't they?" Christina asked, voicing the question all of us wanted to ask but weren't strong enough to say.

Ms. Fleming slowly nodded her head. "I think so."

Christina turned to her brother and asked the same question of him.

"Unless they get some help," he confirmed.

"Help from who?"

"Aren't there whale experts who do this sort of thing?" I volunteered.

"They're called the Whale Stranding Network, but there's no way we can get in touch with anybody . . . can we?"

"Nobody, Mike," Ms. Fleming acknowledged. "But Dr. Resney, or somebody, will be here soon . . . maybe as early as this evening."

"It doesn't matter. They won't survive the day," Mike responded.

"So we have to do it," Christina said.

"Do what?" I asked.

"Save them."

"Us?"

"Us. We're the only ones here so we have to," she said.

"But how? How can we do anything?"

Christina turned to her brother. "Mike?"

He nodded his head slowly. "Their only hope is that we keep 'em wet. And covered up."

"Is that all?" Ms. Fleming asked.

"That and wait for the tide to come back in."

"Mike, we all want to help," Ms. Fleming began, "but we have to be realistic."

"What do you mean, realistic?" he asked suspiciously.

She paused and everybody held their breath waiting for the answer. "I mean we have to look at the situation. There are experts, whale experts, scientists, who are called to help in these circumstances. How can a couple of teachers and a bunch of grade seven students possibly think we can do what they do?"

"Are you saying we just leave them to die?" Christina asked her.

Ms. Fleming opened her mouth to answer when Mike jumped in. "No, we're not going to do that," he said, shaking his head.

"But, Mike —"

"But nothing. We can't just walk away and let

them die." His voice cracked over the last few words. I looked around at the other faces and could see tears in the eyes of more than one person.

"I just don't think we can save them," Ms. Fleming said softly.

A silence enveloped us. I wanted to object, but who could argue with what she had said? Who did we think we were fooling, anyway? The silence was broken by a loud intake of breath from the closest whale.

"I don't know if we can save them . . ." Mike began and then stopped.

"But we can't just walk away without trying," I said, completing his sentence.

He looked over at me and nodded his head. "Yeah. We can't walk away without trying."

Others nodded their heads and voiced agreement. We had to try.

"Please, Ms. Fleming," Christina pleaded.

She nodded her head, and everybody burst into a cheer before Mike silenced them so the whales wouldn't be distressed.

"What do we do?" Ms. Fleming asked.

"We need to keep them wet and to cover them," Mike said.

"Buckets," Ms. Fleming said. "We have to get buckets to haul up water . . . and something to cover them up . . . like . . ."

"Sheets or tablecloths," Christina suggested.

"Exactly!" Ms. Fleming agreed. "Let's get back to the school and gather up all the things we'll need."

"I'm going to stay here," Mike said.

"I can't leave you alone," Ms. Fleming objected.

"I'll stay with him," I volunteered.

"Me too!" Christina said.

"And don't forget about me," Chuckie added.

Ms. Fleming looked hesitant but finally nodded in agreement.

"You all better get the stuff," Mike said. "We can't afford to waste any time."

Ms. Fleming started off, with the rest of the kids trailing behind her. We watched them until they disappeared around the point, then turned our attention back to the whales. We stood helplessly at the edge of the water and watched it slowly slip away. Mike bent down and started to remove his shoes.

"What are you doing?" Christina asked.

"Guess," Mike responded sarcastically. He pulled off his socks as well and waded into the water.

Christina and I exchanged a look. She shrugged, and then the three of us kicked off our shoes and socks. We waded in after Mike. The incline was very slight and I walked in for two dozen metres before the water came up to my knees.

Mike stood beside one of the whales. He reached over and placed his hand on the whale's dorsal fin. The eye of the whale rolled back to try and see where Mike had touched it. I could see fear in its eye. I knew that feeling because I shared it.

"Feel this," Mike directed.

"Are you kidding?" Christina asked.

"No! Feel it. Its back is almost completely dry even though the rest of it's submerged. Try it," Mike said.

Chuckie reached down and touched the whale.

I hesitated.

"Are you afraid, Gord?"

"Of course not," I lied. I couldn't get over how he and Chuckie weren't scared. Reluctantly I reached out and gently placed my hand against the whale. "It feels sort of like . . . I don't know . . ."

"Here, reach under the water and feel its skin there," Mike commanded, taking my hand and pulling it down beneath the surface.

"Rubber! It feels like rubber," I said.

"That's how it's supposed to feel," Mike observed. "You remember when we went to Sea World a few years ago and they let us touch the dolphins?" he asked Christina.

"I didn't get to touch one," she answered. "I left my arm in the pool until it looked like a prune but the dolphins wouldn't come near me."

"That's because you kept fidgeting and talking. The skin is supposed to feel like rubber, like this one does beneath the water. I want to try something."

He bent down and started splashing the whale. Water cascaded down its side, making the skin glisten.

"Come on, give me a hand!" Mike urged us.

I bent down and followed his direction. Christina and Chuckie did the same thing. Water sprayed all across the back of the dorsal fin, showering us as well. Christina stopped.

"Keep going!" Mike ordered.

She shot him a dirty look and then obeyed. I just kept on splashing. I wasn't going to stop until Mike did. He had his head down, his hands cupped, pumping and pumping water up onto the whale's back. My arms were starting to feel tired even though I wasn't working nearly as hard as Mike was. Finally he stopped. He straightened up and reached out to touch the whale.

"Just like I thought! Feel its skin . . . it feels all right again!"

Without warning the whale started to move its gigantic flippers. I jumped back as one of them swept by where I'd just been standing. They broke the surface and water sprayed everywhere.

"What's it doing?" Christina asked. "Did we make it mad?"

Mike shook his head. "I don't think so. Maybe we made it feel better and it's trying to get free. As long as we can get water on them they'll be okay . . . I think. Let's look at another one."

Once again Mike took the lead and we followed behind. He waded in slightly deeper and then parallelled the beach. We were soon standing close, but not too close, to a much smaller whale. Its tail was slowly moving up and down in the water. As we got closer it became more active and started thrashing about.

"It's trying to get free!" Christina said.

We stood by helplessly and watched. The fins continually broke the surface and water was thrown up into the air. I took a step backwards. It was slowly moving, but instead of going into deeper water it was pushing itself farther up the beach.

"This isn't working. It's just getting more stuck.

Can't we turn it around or something?" Christina asked urgently.

"I don't think we can," I replied anxiously. "If we got hit by one of those flippers or trapped underneath it . . ." I let the sentence trail off although I was sure they both knew what I meant. Even a small whale like this one had to weigh ten times as much as one of us.

"But we have to do something," Christina argued.

"He's right. We can't risk it," Mike said, and I felt a sense of relief pass through my whole body. If he'd ordered us to do something I wouldn't have had any choice but to listen to him. "This is just a small one, not much more than a baby, but it still must weigh can awful lot."

"But we have to help it. If we don't, it'll be stranded just like the ones up on the beach," Christina said.

There was a blast of air and spray right behind us and I spun around in time to see another whale break the surface. It was not far out, and unless there was a sudden drop off it couldn't have been in very deep water. Then right beside it another dorsal fin broke the surface. I edged away and into slightly shallower water.

"Why are they hanging around here? They should be going to deeper waters," Christina commented.

"Don't worry about them. They'll be fine, right Mike?" I asked, looking for encouragement.

"I don't know. Sometimes whole pods get stranded . . . hundreds of them."

"But that would happen all at once . . . right?" I was looking for reassurance. Having six or seven stranded was something we could maybe handle, but hundreds?

We stood in silence and watched as yet another whale broke the surface. It exhaled loudly and a spray of water burst into the air. Looking farther out I saw two more whales spy-hopping. I knew we had seven here on the beach, and at least three or four more in the nearby waters, but there was no telling just how many were hidden beneath the surface.

"Look! Here comes everybody!" Christina yelled.

I turned around. The other kids were coming fast and loud.

"Come on," Mike said. He quickly waded through the water, kicking up a spray before him. "Let's talk to them before they get too close."

We ran and met them part way up the beach, just before they'd reached the first whale. We were quickly surrounded by the mob. Most of them were carrying buckets and pots and sheets and towels. Everybody was loud, and there were smiles on their faces. What did they think this was, some sort of party? These whales were going to die without our help, and these kids were acting like this was a joke. We were instantly overwhelmed with questions, too many to understand and respond to.

"Please, everybody be quiet!" Ms. Fleming demanded.

The noise didn't subside, and I figured she couldn't be heard over the commotion.

"Shut up everybody!" Mike shouted.

There was instant silence. He turned to Ms. Fleming. "Tell 'em what you want to tell 'em."

"Thank you. Everybody please sit down."

There was grumbling but kids plopped down, leaving Mike, Christina and me standing beside Ms. Fleming. In the distance I could see Mrs. Murphy and Mrs. Presley trudging up the beach. Even from that distance Mrs. Murphy looked anxious. Mrs. Presley looked angry.

"We have to talk about what we're going to do," Ms. Fleming continued. "Mike, could you explain what you know about these whales and how you think we might help?"

"I'm not sure," he said hesitantly. His reluctance caught me by surprise. He had been so much in charge, and knew so much.

"Could you just tell us what you know about these whales and stranding situations?" she asked.

"I don't know. I don't know much," he answered, staring down, digging the toes of one bare foot into the hardened sand.

"Please, Mike, you're the only one with any information."

"Come on, Mike," Christina urged.

He nodded his head slowly. "We gotta keep 'em wet, that's the most important thing. Wet and covered. If they dry out, or get sunburned, they'll die."

I suddenly became aware of the sun shining brightly. It was getting hot and warm and there wasn't a cloud in the sky to offer even the hope of shade.

"We also have to make sure when we drape the covers over them that we don't cover their blowholes and —"

"What's a blowhole?" somebody asked.

"It's like their nose except it's on their backs. That has to be kept free."

"I'm not getting too close," someone objected. "They could bite."

"You don't have to be afraid. They only eat small fish and squid," I offered, regurgitating the information Mike had given me only minutes earlier.

Mrs. Murphy and Mrs. Presley stopped and stood behind the last row of kids sitting on the sand.

"But so what if we keep them wet?" somebody asked. "That isn't going to get them back into the water."

"No, but it'll keep them alive until the water comes back for them. High tide will be here by nine-fifteen or nine-thirty this evening," Ms. Fleming answered.

"So all we have to do until then is sort of wet them down?" Jenna asked.

"That's all, and then the tide will do the rest. Right, Mike?" Ms. Fleming asked.

"I guess so," he replied. He didn't sound very confident, and that troubled me.

"Okay. There are forty-nine students, and of course three adults. How many whales are there?"

"Seven," I answered. "And at least a couple more are fooling around in the shallows."

"All right. We have to pair off, and then we'll assign the pairs to a specific whale. You'll need to take sheets and towels and buckets," Ms. Fleming directed. "Once you get the sheet wet you drape it over part of the whale. It's like a sunscreen."

"I hope you know you're going to be responsible for all this damage. These sheets and towels will only be fit for the garbage!" Mrs. Presley said angrily.

"We'll be responsible," Ms. Fleming assured her.

Mrs. Presley turned to Mrs. Murphy, who nodded in agreement.

"It's a waste of your time, and my linen," Mrs. Presley continued.

"What do you mean?" Ms. Fleming asked.

"Strandings happen all the time. It's nature's way, and there's nothing you can do about it," she replied.

Her words left everybody sitting in silence. Were we fighting a battle we couldn't win? How could we possibly do anything? The nearest whale loudly exhaled. We all turned to face it. I saw it rise as its lungs filled with air. There was a rumbling of responses.

"Well . . ." Mrs. Presley said. "I guess you have to do something to try to save the poor things. I'm going to go back up to the school and make sandwiches . . ." She paused. "No, not sandwiches. What you need is something hot . . . like soup or stew. That water is chilly and it's going to sap away your warmth and energy." She paused again and I could see she was thinking. "If I had some help, I could fix something better."

"That would be wonderful!" Ms. Fleming gushed. "How much help do you need?"

"Four or five strong kids should do it. I need them to gather driftwood and then cut it into smaller pieces."

"Cut it? With what?" Mrs. Murphy asked with alarm.

"Axes, unless they have sharp teeth," Mrs. Presley replied.

"Axes?" Mrs. Murphy said with alarm. She shook her head slowly. "Well . . . it'll be fine as long as I'm right there to supervise. Are you all right without me?" she asked Ms. Fleming.

"We'll be fine. You go back with Mrs. Presley now and get things ready and I'll sort out which kids will go back to the school."

Mrs. Murphy nodded. She moved over to Ms. Fleming's side. "Please watch them carefully," she said softly.

"I'll do my best."

Mrs. Murphy turned and walked away with Mrs. Presley. Kids started to get up from the sand.

"Sit down!" Ms. Fleming ordered. Reluctantly, everybody complied. "We need to plan this out."

"We need to get moving," Mike said forcefully.

"We do need to get moving, but moving in the right direction," she countered. "Be patient. Now, is there anybody who's nervous around animals . . . anybody who'd rather not get too close to the whales?"

One hand slowly rose, followed by a second and a third. Two girls and a boy, all from the other class. I had wanted to raise my hand too, but I was too afraid to acknowledge that I was nervous.

"I'd like you three to go back to the school and help there, okay?"

Thank goodness I hadn't raised my hand!

They rose and started across the beach.

"Is there anybody here who isn't confident in the water?" Ms. Fleming asked.

A couple of hands, then three more, and finally a sixth, rose into the air.

"All right, I want the six of you to pair up with a more experienced partner. As well, I want the rest of you to get yourselves a buddy, right now."

Kids scrambled to get somebody to be their partner. Mike and Chuckie hooked up leaving me to find somebody else. I scanned the crowd but didn't see anybody free who I knew well enough to ask. Then I locked eyes with Christina. She pointed to herself and then to me, which I took to mean she was asking if we could be partners. I nodded my head.

"When you've found your buddy please sit back down," Ms. Fleming ordered. "Come on, hurry up, the whales are waiting."

People flopped back down to the sand. Ms. Fleming started pairing up the few remaining stragglers.

There was a loud spout as a whale broke to the surface just out from us. As we all stood by, awestruck, and watched, the whale struggled forward and forced its way into the shallow water. Its powerful tail repeatedly broke the surface, smashing loudly, throwing up spray, propelling it farther forward. Right in front of our eyes another whale was beaching itself! Seeing them on the beach was unreal enough, but watching it happen was beyond belief. It was like the difference between driving by a car accident on the side of the road and actually watching it happen.

"I don't understand what's happening. The storm's passed and the waves aren't that big. I don't know why it would beach itself," Ms. Fleming cried out in confusion.

"And I think there might be more coming," Mike added. "I've been watching. There are a lot more whales out there in the bay and they keep coming in close and then swimming out again."

"We can't do anything about that, or even worry about it," Ms. Fleming replied. "For now I want six people, three sets of buddies, to go to each whale. Take buckets and sheets. Are you sure about covering them, Mike?"

He nodded. "Yeah, just don't cover the blowhole."

"Everybody understand?" Ms. Fleming asked. "Anything else, Mike?"

"Yeah, don't yell or talk too loud, and try not to touch them too much."

"Okay, let's go."

A ripple of raw energy and excitement pushed us along as kids started to spread out across the sand and into the shallows. Christina handed me one of the two buckets she'd picked up. We ran along with the wave of kids to the water's edge and quickly filled them. They swelled with the weight of the water, but I felt so charged it felt like nothing.

"Which one?" she asked.

"I think that one," I answered, pointing inland to where the largest lay, farthest from the water's edge. "It needs the most help."

We were only part way there when I saw that Chuckie and Mike were thinking the exact same thing. We met on our way up the beach and quickly moved together to the whale's side. We stopped and stared at the animal. Jenna and Lauren joined us to make three pairs.

It was, by far, the biggest whale on the beach. It was close to 6 metres long and must have weighed more than a car. Its dorsal fin stood almost at my eye level and its two flippers extended well out from its body. It was probably just a trick of the light, but it seemed to be much darker in colour than the other whales. It was motionless, and its eyes were closed.

"Are you sure we're not already too late?" Chuckie asked. "Like maybe it's already . . . you know . . . gone."

"It's definitely not *gone*, Chuckie," Christina replied. "Although it may be dead. Mike?"

"I don't know. None of them seem to breathe very often. Chuckie, help me drape the sheets over it and the rest of you go and get the extra buckets full of water."

I picked up a second bucket, as did Christina and the other pair. We ran down to the water's edge. Hitting it at full speed I staggered and almost fell over. I righted myself in time before plunging totally under. I splashed into the water and filled the buckets. They were heavy — much heavier than the first, when I'd only carried one — and I struggled under the weight. Water spilled out as they bumped against my legs while I climbed the gentle incline of the beach, back to the whale.

"I think we should call him Captain," Christina said.

"The whale?"

"Yeah. Mike said they're pilot whales, and pilots are usually called Captain. Don't you think that's a good name?"

"I guess so . . . I just hadn't thought about naming him."

By the time we reached Captain, he was partially draped with sheets. It was obvious he was alive. He was reacting to the cover being placed on him. Rather than simply lying motionless, his massive tail was moving up and down. Up close I noticed his eyes were open and he was trying to peer back to see us. There was a stream of liquid, like tears, flowing from his eye.

"Here," Mike called, taking the first bucket from his sister. He walked to the head of the whale and gently poured it. The water ran down the whale's head, and some of it flowed into his eyes. I handed him one of the buckets I was carrying and he did the same thing again. Christina poured her other bucket on top of one of the sheets and it became plastered to the creature's back. I followed suit and poured my other bucket in such a way that the one sheet was completely soaked.

"Did you hear that?" Mike asked.

"What? I don't hear anything," Chuckie answered.

"Listen!" Mike commanded.

We all closed our mouths and opened our ears. I heard the sounds of kids laughing and talking, and the wind and the constant background sounds of the waves against the shore, and . . . something else. It was a high-pitched whine. It was unmistakably coming from our whale. I stepped back. It was an eerie, haunting sound that sent a shiver down my spine.

"The poor thing! He's crying out in pain!" Christina said.

"No. I think he's talking to the other whales."

Chuckie wasn't buying that. "Come on, Mike, talking?"

"Yeah. Not like we talk —"

"That's for sure, the whales probably make more sense than you two," Christina interrupted.

"Shut up," Mike said. "Whales talk to each other. Don't you ever watch reruns of *Flipper*?"

"Yeah, yeah, for sure!" Chuckie said enthusiastically. "Flipper made all sorts of squeaks and chirps."

"That's right, and that's how they communi—" Mike stopped. "Listen!"

There were more high-pitched sounds, but this time they were clearly not coming from "our" whale.

"Somebody else is trying to say something," Christina said.

"Probably asking for water. Chuckie and me will haul up some more water," Mike said, taking the bucket from my hand.

I moved toward the head of the whale. As I moved, his eye followed me. It gave me a strange feeling. I wondered what he was thinking . . . did he know we were trying to help, or —?

"Poor thing. I wonder what he's thinking," Christina said, reading my mind.

"I don't know."

"He must be trying to figure us out. Some scientists

think they may be even smarter than chimpanzees and apes. He's probably scared," she said.

"Do you think so?"

"Yeah. Wouldn't you be scared if you were out of your element and away from your family and surrounded by things you don't know anything about? Wouldn't that be scary?"

Yeah, it is scary, I thought, but I didn't say anything.

TUESDAY 12:45 P.M.

I'd been up and down the beach so many times I'd lost count long ago and I was feeling the strain in both my arms and legs. I knew I wasn't moving nearly as fast, but I wasn't surprised. In fact, after the limited sleep and all the excitement of last night I figured I should have been more beat. I looked at the others doing the same thing and realized they had slowed down considerably as well. What had started with such energy and enthusiasm just a few hours before had bogged down. A few kids were sitting down, while others seemed to be almost aimlessly wandering instead of doing the jobs they'd been assigned. I had to fight the urge to sit down myself, at least for a few minutes.

"What do you think you're doing?"

I turned in the direction of the voice. It was Mike, standing over top of two of the kids who were resting.

"Get up!" he yelled. I could see one of the kids answering but was too far away to hear his response. What I could see was that neither of them moved. Suddenly Mike reached down and grabbed one of the guys by the shirt and pulled him to his feet.

"Mike!" Ms. Fleming called out as she rushed toward him. Mike released his grip on the kid. I set my buckets down in the sand and the muscles in my arms relaxed. I needed to get closer to hear what was going to happen.

"Mike, some of the kids need to take a breather."

"We don't have time for anybody to rest!" he answered. "The whales need us!"

"You must be tired too. Why don't I have every-body take a short break," she suggested.

"I don't need a break!" he answered defiantly. He turned away from her and looked directly at me. "Do you need a break?" he demanded of me.

I shook my head frantically. "No . . . I don't need a break," I stammered.

"Good!" he said. "Some of us are going to keep working!" he yelled over his shoulder as he marched back to the water's edge. "Come on, Gord," he said as he brushed by me. I turned and followed. My aching arms and sore back would have to wait.

12:55 P.M.

Walking up and down the beach carrying the buckets, my mind kept drifting back to the activities of last night. It all seemed like a strange dream, or nightmare

— wandering around an isolated island in the dead of night in a rainstorm and being confronted by an old man. And despite what Chuckie believed, I knew we hadn't seen a ghost. It was a man, a very old and angry man, but a man. I wondered if he'd show up at the school today and complain about us being there. Or maybe do something worse.

With each trip I had more time to think because the distance was becoming greater as the tide continued to go out. As well, the walk would continue to grow over the next three hours until the tide finally turned.

At first I'd felt jealous of the groups working on whales still partially submerged; they didn't have to haul water up the beach. But after I'd made a few trips down to get water I realized how chilly it was. There were little clusters of kids sitting on the sand, shaking from the cold.

I heard a loud spray and turned to the sound. A large whale was making a pass parallel to the shore. It turned and came in even closer. I feared what was going to happen next — what had happened six times already over the last few hours. Just like the others, this whale suddenly turned directly toward the beach. Breaking through the shallow waters it propelled itself forward. I watched in helpless amazement, as did the others, who'd also stopped working to witness the spectacle. Its tail thrashed up and down while the fins cut through the water throwing spray high into the air. It rode a wave, which crashed onto the beach. As the wave receded, the whale was left, resting on the sand, almost completely out of the water. The next wave crashed up and over the whale and I held my breath, hoping against hope that it would some- how drag the animal back out to sea. As the wave disappeared, the whale remained.

And worse yet, with the receding water, my hope felt like it had been drained away as well.

With each new whale, pairs of kids had to leave the whale they'd been working on to try to help the newest stranding. People were reluctant to start working with the newer whales. Each group had named their whale and were getting attached to it. I had to laugh at some of the names — there was Shadow, Winnie the Whale, Oreo, Tofu, Wave, Echo, and the littlest one, who was chocolaty brown, was named Pudding. Christina bris- tled at any suggestion we stop working with Captain, saying she'd never abandon "her whale."

I waded into the water and dipped both buckets beneath the waves to fill them. Pulling them up, I felt the strain of the weight.

I turned and started back up the beach. Christina was slightly ahead of me. She was just as determined as Mike. I picked up my pace to catch up with her. She nodded her head but didn't say anything. We walked side by side to Captain and handed our buckets to Mike and Chuckie. They poured them over top of the whale.

Mike looked over at me. "He's not doing so good," he said softly.

"He's doing just fine!" Christina objected.

Mike shook his head sadly. "He's not breathing as often . . . hasn't moved at all for fifteen minutes . . . or opened his eyes."

"And the colour's changing. He's getting blacker," Chuckie noted.

"Don't be ridiculous! Why would his colour change? And even if it was, it might mean he's getting better," Christina protested.

"Nope. I think things are getting worse," Mike commented.

"Then we have to get more water or more sheets or something!" Christina said. There was a catch in her voice, like she was fighting back tears.

"It's not that. We're keeping him wet. There's something else that needs to be done that we're not doing," Mike said.

"What? What do we have to do?" Christina demanded.

"I don't know. I just know we need to do something else."

"Well figure it out," she insisted. "Figure it out!"

I reached down and picked up one of the water bottles that had been brought down for us to drink from. It was empty, and I dropped it to the sand. I picked up another one and shook it. It was empty as well.

"We need drinking water," I commented.

"What?" Mike demanded, turning around to face me. "What did you say?"

"Drinking water . . . we need drinking water," I answered sheepishly.

"Exactly! Exactly! That's what's wrong. We're pouring water *on* them but we need to pour some *in* them!"

"We have to give them a drink?" Chuckie asked, confused.

"Yes, that's what we have to do!"

"Sure, but how do we do it?" I asked.

"I don't know . . . but we have to figure it out."

"How's it going, guys?"

I turned around to see Ms. Fleming. Looking past her, I saw that kids were abandoning their buckets and walking up the beach toward the school.

"I don't think he's doing very well," Mike answered.

"He's doing fine!" Christina jumped in.

"I was asking about the four of you . . . are you guys doing okay?"

"Yeah, no problem," Mike answered. He started to walk away to get more water. Then he saw that nobody was working with the whales. He spun back around.

"Why did everybody stop?" he demanded.

"It's time for lunch . . . everybody's going up to the school for lunch," Ms. Fleming said.

"They can't do that! They have to stay here to help the whales!"

"They need to eat, to take a rest . . . *you* need to eat. You can't keep working non-stop for twelve hours," she explained.

"Maybe you can't, but I can," Mike objected.

"Come on Mike, it's time. You won't be gone long. Just long enough to grab a warm meal and get into some dry clothing."

"No," he answered and turned back for the water.

Ms. Fleming looked surprised and shocked.

"Do you want me to talk to him?" Christina asked.

Ms. Fleming shook her head. "I'll do it. Chuckie, are you his partner?"

"Yeah."

"You stay with me. Christina and Gordon, go and join the others."

I happily abandoned my empty bucket, dropping it to the sand, grateful that I'd been ordered to leave. I started up the beach, but stopped after a couple of steps when I realized Christina wasn't coming.

"He'll be fine," I called out to her. She looked worried but came toward me, and we rushed to catch up to the crowd of kids who were already well ahead of us.

"Wait!" Ms. Fleming called out.

We stopped. She walked toward us. Chuckie continued on down to the water's edge, where I could see Mike was already filling his two buckets.

"I want you two to go straight to the school with the others. I don't want any hanky-panky," she said.

"You don't understand!" I protested. I don't know what bothered me more — being accused of something I hadn't done or having to admit reluctantly to myself that I *did* like her.

"I understand very well. I can remember what it was like to be twelve or thirteen years old."

"Don't worry, Ms. Fleming, we'll go straight up to the school," Christina replied.

"Good! Thank you, Christina. I'll be up shortly myself, either with or without your brother, and Chuckie."

The last few stragglers were just disappearing around the point. We walked quickly after them without exchanging a word.

1:20 P.M.

In the distance I saw a column of smoke rising up into the cloudless sky. Then, as we got closer, the unmistakable smell of a fire reached my nostrils. I love a fire! Putting in the kindling just the right way, throwing in balled-up pieces of newspaper, watching the fire get started and the flames licking at the fuel until it catches and spreads — then sitting around watching it, poking it with the fireplace tools, sending sparks flying and roasting marshmallows and . . . but of course that was in our old house . . . the place where we lived now didn't even have a fireplace . . . or a lot of other things, either.

"That smells good," Christina said.

"Um . . . yeah. I like the smell of a fire too."

"I wasn't talking about the fire. I mean the food. I can smell lunch."

Up ahead we could see the fire blazing. How wonderful it would have been to just stand there and warm myself — if only there'd been time. Atop the fire, held by a spit, sat a large cooking pot. A line of kids was off to the side of the pot, bowls in hand, and Mrs. Presley was spooning out servings of stew. I inhaled deeply. It smelled wonderful.

Christina and I joined the end of the line. There was a stack of bowls. I picked one up and handed it to Christina. She thanked me and I took one for myself. The line moved quickly and we were soon at the front.

"This will warm you up," Mrs. Presley said as he scooped out heaping servings first to Christina and then into my bowl. "You can find rolls and drinks in the dining room."

Christina and I carried our food inside. Although it was filled with kids there were practically no sounds. Everybody was huddled over their food and ate in silence. I figured they were as tired and hungry as I was. We took seats at the table where Jenna and Lauren were already eating. We all exchanged greetings and made small talk. The stew smelled wonderful and I eagerly dug in. The warmth slid down my throat and I felt my stomach start to glow.

I looked up to see Ms. Fleming enter the room. She was alone. She scanned the room, looking for something. We locked eyes and she shook her head, which I took to mean that Mike and Chuckie weren't coming. She walked slowly to the front of the room, looking worn and tired.

"Could everybody stop eating for a minute!" she called out.

People turned in their seats and put down their forks.

"It's almost one-thirty. You've all been working hard . . . very hard, for almost three hours. The tide will be continuing to go out for more than another hour and a half. We hope no more whales will be stranded in that time."

I knew this was a false hope. There were at least four whales swimming through the shallows who seemed determined to join the others on the beach. What were they doing? What was driving these creatures?

"I know we're all tired but we have to keep going. Remember that in ninety minutes help will arrive."

"Help?" somebody questioned. "Dr. Resney is coming to help us?"

"I don't know," she answered softly. "Maybe people will arrive, but I just don't know. We still can't radio out or receive messages in. We don't know, although it can't be much longer."

"Then what did you mean by help?" Jenna asked.

"The tide. In about ninety minutes the tide will start to rise again. All we have to do is keep the whales wet and the tide will come up and rescue them. And each time a whale floats away it'll free more kids to help with the remaining whales."

"When will high tide arrive?" somebody asked.

"Sometime after nine tonight," Ms. Fleming replied. "We'll all keep working, but first you all need to eat, change into something dry and then get back down to the beach."

Christina turned to me. "Captain won't be back in the water for almost eight more hours." She paused and her brow furrowed. "Is he going to make it?"

"I don't know . . . I just don't know . . ."

I looked away and caught sight of Ms. Fleming motioning for me.

"Come on," I said to Christina.

We rose from our seats and walked to the front.

"Mike refused to come up so I had to leave Chuckie with him. I told him I'd have somebody bring down food for them. Can you two please do that?"

"Yeah, no problem," I answered.

"Ms. Fleming, did Mike talk to you about getting the whales a drink?" Christina asked.

"He mentioned something about it, but I don't have any idea how to do it. Do either of you have any suggestions?"

"None," I admitted. Christina shook her head.

"If only we had somebody to turn to. Poor Mike, he feels like he's letting the whales down because he doesn't know what to do. *I* don't even know what to do. If only we had an expert." She paused. "You two had better finish eating and then get back down to the beach. Don't forget to bring something for the boys, okay?"

We nodded in agreement and Ms. Fleming walked off.

"You still hungry?" Christina asked.

"No, not really," I said. "We should get changed, grab food for the guys and head back down."

We went off to our rooms. I hurried and moved as quickly as I could, but when I returned to the dining room Christina was already at the buffet table loading up.

"What do they like?" I asked.

"Everything. Just take lots of everything. Get bread, butter, dessert . . . everything. And we'll get them some stew. But how are we going to get it all down to them?"

"Maybe we can ask Mrs. Presley to put the food in a container or something," I suggested.

"Good idea. Come on, let's go out and ask her."

Christina pushed through the door, and I followed right behind. Mrs. Presley was standing by the fire, stirring the still-bubbling stew. Two kids were walking away with overflowing bowls.

"Back for seconds are you?" she asked.

"No, we have to bring some food back down to the beach for my brother and his friend. We need something we can carry it in."

"Forget the beach, have them come up here to eat," she replied.

"They couldn't come. They had to stay down there to watch the whales," Christina explained.

"Oh . . . oh . . . okay. I'll pack them up a meal. Can one of you keep stirring this pot for me?" she asked.

"I'll do it," Christina offered.

"No," I said as I stepped forward and took the long-handled spoon. "I'll do it. You look beat, go and sit down." I pointed toward a stump just over to the side. She looked like she was going to argue at first, but she stopped herself and took a seat.

"Pretty gentlemanly of you, young fella," Mrs. Presley noted.

"What?" I questioned.

"Don't see many boys treat girls like ladies. Are you two sweet on each other?"

"No! I was just . . . just being polite," I objected strongly.

"Really? Looks to me like you like each other."

"No, we don't," I objected.

"Whatever you say, son. I'll be back in a minute."
She walked away to the school.

"Why don't you like me?" Christina asked.

"I *do* like you," I answered.

"Then why did you tell her you didn't?"

"I meant, like, we aren't, you know, going around
together. Why do people keep thinking we are?"

"I guess because we're talking and are together
and things," Christina answered.

"It's so embarrassing," I muttered.

"It's embarrassing for people to think that you
might like me? What's wrong with me?" she
demanded.

"Nothing's wrong with you! *Nothing*!" I felt a
flush come over my whole body and my palms felt
sweaty. "And I *do* like you," I reluctantly admitted.
"Do you like me?" I didn't even know where that
question had come from.

"Yeah, sure, you're all right . . . I guess."

Mrs. Presley came back carrying two large plastic
containers. I was so happy to see her because it meant
our conversation was over.

"I'll put in two big helpings."

She and Christina started to talk while she filled
the containers. I wasn't paying any attention, though.
My mind was spinning around, thinking about the
whales, and Mike and Chuckie down on the beach,
and the things Christina and I had just talked about.

"Is there anything else I can get you?" Mrs. Presley
asked.

"A whale expert would be nice," I suggested.

"Shame the Resneys aren't here . . . they know so much about all marine life."

"I hope everything is all right," Christina said.

"I'm sure things are fine," Mrs. Presley offered.

"Everything would be so different if they were still here," I commented. "Then we wouldn't be relying on a thirteen-year-old to be the only one on the island who knows anything about whales."

"He's not the only one," Mrs. Presley said.

"Well, yeah, I know the teachers know something," I replied.

"And you too," Christina offered to Mrs. Presley.

"Me? Heavens no, I don't know hardly a thing. I was thinking of somebody else."

"Who?" I asked.

"Old man Amos," she said.

"The ghost from the story?" I asked, swallowing hard.

"Heavens no, he's far from a ghost. He's an old man. He lives in a little rundown house on the other side of the island."

I swallowed even harder. "Beside the lighthouse?"

"Yep, that's the place."

"I thought this whole island was a state park. Why do they allow anybody to live here?" Christina asked.

"They don't have much choice. His father and grandfather and his great-great-uncle before that lived on the island. Wasn't always a state park. There used to be a whole village out here and a whaling station."

"A whole village!" I echoed in amazement.

"Not a big village. Just ten or twelve houses. Eventually all the people moved away or were bought out to make way for the park. Once they left, the houses were torn down to return the island to its natural state."

"Why hasn't he left?" Christina asked.

"He didn't want to go and they didn't make him. It's only one small house and they figure he'll die soon enough."

"Is he sick?"

"No, just old . . . I'm not sure how old . . . somewhere in his mid-eighties."

"Wow, that *is* old!" I exclaimed.

"Sure is, but just because he's old don't mean he's going to die none too soon. That old man is too tough and stubborn to die. He knows they're just waiting for him to kick off, so he's sworn he's going to outlive all the politicians and civil servants. Said he's going to live to see them all put into the ground."

"And he knows about whales?" Christina asked.

"He does."

"Is he a marine biologist?" I asked.

"Hah! That he's not, but he knows about whales . . . the way a cat knows about mice."

"I don't know what you mean," I said.

"He's a whaler, or at least he was a whaler when he was young and the laws were different."

"That's disgusting! Killing whales is inhumane!" Christina exclaimed.

"Don't think anybody thinks it's right any more," Mrs. Presley added.

"How could anybody do such a thing? How could somebody be so cruel?" Christina questioned.

"Now just hold on there, young lady! My father, rest his soul in heaven, was a whaler, and he was one of the kindest and gentlest men who ever walked upon the earth! Don't go judging the past by the present. Those were different times and things were seen differently!"

"I didn't mean anything bad about your father," Christina apologized.

Mrs. Presley gave a big sigh. "It's me who should be apologizing to you for getting myself so steamed up."

Christina gave her a smile in response. "Do you think you could ask him to help us with the whales?"

"Me ask that old buzzard for help? It would be a frosty day in . . .." She stopped and looked all embarrassed. "I'm never going to ask him for anything."

"But it's important, Mrs. Presley," Christina pleaded.

"Important or not, or whether I ask or not, doesn't really matter. He's not what you'd call a friendly old man, especially to anybody who works here. He figures the reason he's being kicked off the island is because of the school." She paused. "I've got to get started on supper so you two better get running along. Get this meal down to the beach before it gets all cold." She handed Christina a bag containing the containers of stew.

"Thanks a lot, Mrs. Presley," Christina said.

"Yeah, thanks," I echoed.

We started back for the beach.

"This old man, Mr. Amos, is he the guy you ran into last night?" Christina asked.

"We didn't stop to ask him his name, but who else could it have been?"

"So you know where his house is, right?"

"Of course I do. It's right by the light . . ." I stopped. "No! We're not going to see that old man!"

"How else can we get him to help?"

"We can't! Weren't you listening to what Mrs. Presley said? He isn't going to help us, and besides, I'm not going to help you get there."

"Who needs your help! You don't think I can find a lighthouse on my own? Here, take this!" she said, slamming the bag holding the lunches into my hands.

She turned and strode away. I stood there with my mouth open and watched her walk away.

"You two have a little spat?"

I turned around. Jenna was standing there with a big smile on her face.

I pressed the lunch into her hands. "Here, take this and give it to Chuckie and Mike." I ran after her.

TUESDAY 1:55 P.M.

I scrambled across the sand to catch up to her. She was already halfway up the sand dune behind the school. I hit the base of the hill and clambered up on all fours. I caught up to her before she'd reached the top of the rise. She looked over and flashed a smile.

"Wait a second," I panted, out of breath.

I shielded my eyes with my hand and turned to look around. From the top of the dune, the lighthouse was clearly visible in the distance. In fact, from this height I could see the wide expanse of the island. Except for the school, the lighthouse and the small house beside it, all I could see were sand, scrub bush and tall dune grass, blowing in the wind.

"Did you come up here to sightsee or what?" Christina asked.

"To come with you."

"Then don't you think we'd better get moving?"

I took a bearing toward the lighthouse and we skied down the side of the dune. Sand sprayed up and got into the few remaining places it hadn't gotten into on the trip up the other side. At least the sand was warm and dry. *Nothing like last night*, I thought.

Last night! A wave of anxiety hit me. This wasn't just a stroll through the dunes. We were going to talk to some cantankerous old man. The little bit he'd said the night before was mostly spoken by that thing he was waving around. Was it a gun, and did he really fire at us? Or was I just imagining the whole thing? I didn't know what we were going to say to him.

"When we get there, let me do most of the talking," Christina said, as if she were reading my mind.

"I have a better idea," I countered. "How about if you do *all* of the talking."

She smiled. "Sounds like you're scared."

"Well, he didn't take a shot at you."

She stopped and grabbed me by the arm. "He did what?"

"Shot at us."

"Are you sure?"

"Well . . . yeah . . . I guess," I mumbled.

"You guess? Come on, if somebody tried to shoot me I'd know it. What happened?"

"It's all confusing. It was dark and it happened so fast . . ."

"And?"

"He had something in his arms . . . it could have been a gun . . . and then when we were running away I heard something . . . it sounded like a gunshot."

"And you think he tried to hit you?"

"I don't know. You wouldn't believe how loud it sounded. It made me jump." Boy was I sounding like a wimp. "It made us all jump, even Mike," I added, so she'd know it wasn't just me who was scared.

"I guess you can't really blame him," Christina said.

"What do you mean?"

"Poor old man. Out here all by himself and he hears a noise and finds three strange kids by his house. He probably thought you were trying to break in. You must have scared him half to death!"

"Scared *him*?" I asked in disbelief.

"That's right. Wouldn't you be scared if somebody tried to break into your house when you were alone in the middle of the night?"

"I'm never alone at night."

"Don't get silly about this. The first thing you should do when we get there is apologize," she suggested.

"No way I'm going to do that. If I apologize he'll know I was one of the kids. It's better that he doesn't know, or he might not help us."

She didn't say anything in response, which I took as agreement.

"Chuckie told me you live with your mother," Christina said, completely changing the direction of the conversation.

"Well, yeah . . . sort of."

"Sort of? What does that mean?" she asked.

"I live with my mother right now."

"Oh, I understand . . . you're going to move in with your father soon," she reasoned.

"No, I'm not going to leave my mother. My father'll be moving back . . . soon, I'm sure."

"That's good. You must be pretty happy about that. When's he moving back in?"

"Well . . . they haven't set a date yet . . . but soon," I mumbled.

"I see," she replied.

I could tell by the way she said those words that she didn't believe what I was saying. I wanted to change the topic. "Can I ask you a question?"

"Yeah, sure."

"Why doesn't your brother like me?"

"He likes you okay, I guess. He hasn't hit you, has he?"

"No! Of course not!" I answered in alarm.

"Then at least he doesn't *not* like you."

"I'm confused. What do you mean?"

"If he didn't like you he would have popped you. Mike isn't that friendly with very many people. Used to be he hung around mainly with Chuckie. And that's not always been too good for either of them."

"Why?" I asked, although I had a pretty good idea after seeing them together.

"They get in trouble. Mike calls it being creative. I figure it's more than coincidence that they were put in different classes and have different lunch periods this year," she explained. "Mainly the two of them only see each other after school and on weekends."

She paused and a look of concern crossed her

face. "But you know, even Chuckie hasn't been coming over to the house as often the last couple of weeks. I wonder why."

I knew the answer. Chuckie had been over to my place a lot, especially in the last week because we were working on a school project together. Is that why Mike didn't like me?

Before I could play that idea out any more we moved around another dune and the house and lighthouse were right in front of us, along a flat section of sand. I studied the house as we continued to walk. It was two storeys tall, white clapboard siding, red roof with a weathervane at the top, gingerbread on the eaves. A large porch fronted the house and circled around out of view, wrapping around the building.

My mind was filled with images, both from last night and from the story Dr. Resney had told. They blurred together and I had to remind myself I'd only seen an old man and not three mutilated bodies, and that he was a man and not a ghost.

As we moved closer, my lunch, which had gone down so wonderfully, formed into a solid ball in the pit of my stomach. I didn't want to do this — I *really* didn't want to do this. I tried to think of some way out, but knew I couldn't leave — not without looking like the biggest loser and coward in the universe.

Up close the house was more rundown than it was scary. The white paint was peeling and flaking off the clapboard, pieces of the gingerbread were missing, a section of eavestrough hung down limply, almost half the spindles on the railing were gone, and one of the front windows was broken, a piece of cardboard taped to the glass.

I hesitated at the steps. Christina went forward and then stopped, turning to face me.

"Well?"

"Nothing," I answered. I bounded up the steps to join her on unsteady legs.

The wooden floor creaked and groaned under our feet. I tried to walk more softly but to no avail — it kept announcing our arrival. Christina pulled open the screen door. It squeaked like every door in every horror movie I'd ever seen. She raised her hand and knocked. I held my breath and waited . . . and waited.

"I guess he can't hear me . . . he's old and probably hard of hearing. My grandmother is like that," Christina explained.

She knocked again. This time much more loudly. I perked my ears, straining to hear any response from inside — a voice, a groan, the sound of movement, something. There was nothing. Christina reached out, turned the doorknob and pushed open the door. My eyes widened in surprise.

"What are you doing?" I demanded in amazement.

"What does it look like?" She pushed the door open farther and leaned into the house. "HEEELLL-LOOOO!"

Her action caught me totally unprepared. Thank goodness there was still no response. He wasn't there, and we could go now and we'd have done the right thing and . . . Christina stepped into the house and the screen door closed behind her. My jaw almost dropped to the floor. Was she crazy?

"HEELLOO!" She turned around and looked at me through the screen door. "I wonder where he is?"

"I don't know," I stammered, "but you can't do that."

"Do what . . . step into his house?" she asked.

I nodded. "Just think how mad he got yesterday when we only walked on the porch. We have to get out of here!"

"We can't just go . . . what if something has happened to him?"

"Happened to him? What do you mean?"

"He's an old man, maybe it's like in those commercials. You know, 'I've fallen and I can't get up.' Maybe he had a heart attack when the three of you scared him last night."

"It was him who scared us!"

"He might be hurt. We have to check."

"What are you suggesting?" I asked with alarm.

"We have to go in and look around."

"You're crazy!" I practically shouted, before I realized I should be keeping my voice down. "You can't just walk into somebody's house," I said, in a whisper.

"You can't just walk away, knowing somebody might need your help," Christina countered. "I'm going inside."

Before I could even think to argue she'd disappeared into the darkened entrance.

Without thinking I stepped forward and grabbed the screen door. I pulled it open and then let it clank shut without entering.

"This is crazy!" I said out loud. "Just crazy! You can't just walk into somebody's house! It's wrong . . . it's illegal . . . it's . . . oh, what the heck!" I grabbed the door once again, pulled it open and stepped inside.

It was dark; the only light was shining in from behind me. The little I could see was a hallway stretching out in front of me. The air was damp and smelled musty and foul. I took a few tentative steps down the hall. My eyes were slow to adjust to the dim light. I put one hand on the wall to guide me and moved forward.

"Christina?" I called out softly.

"Yeah," she called from behind me.

I jumped straight up into the air and spun in midair.

"How did you . . . ?"

"I was looking in that room first," she answered, pointing to a darkened room tucked just inside the front door.

"Come on," she said, gently brushing by me to go farther down the hall. "Mr. Amos?" She took a few more steps. "Mr. Amos?" she called more loudly.

I crowded in behind Christina. We walked into what looked like a living room. It was even darker than the hall. There was only a thin line of light leaking in around the closed blinds. The room held a couple of chesterfields, some chairs and a couple of end tables. Even in the semi-darkness I could see the room was filled with clutter: books and magazines, little figurines and bric-a-brac covered the tables. The air was dusty and tickled my nose and throat. I had to fight not to sneeze. There was the sound of a clock ticking and I scanned the room until I located it, sitting among a collection of papers on the fireplace mantel.

"Mr. Amos?" Christina called out.

She startled me when she spoke and I jumped slightly to the side.

"I wish you'd stop jumping like that, you're making me nervous!" she hissed through clenched teeth.

"Good, then I'm not alone being scared," I replied, shocked by my admission of fear. I lowered my voice. "Let's get out of here."

She shot me a look that glared through the dim light. I turned away and something in the corner of the room caught my eye. There, lying on an old lounger chair, was a man. He wasn't moving, and I thought, although I couldn't be sure, that his eyes were closed. I raised my hand and pointed.

"There he is," I whispered.

We stared for a few seconds. He didn't move.

"Is he asleep?" I asked quietly.

"Or . . . or . . . ?"

She didn't need to complete the question for me to know what she was thinking, because I was thinking the same thing.

"Mr. Amos?" she called out.

He didn't answer or stir.

"Go over there," she whispered.

"What?"

"Go over there," she repeated.

"Me?"

She nodded her head.

"And do what?" I asked.

"Give him a shake or something." She pushed me from behind, propelling me forward.

If coming to the house was stupid, and walking in the door was crazy, this was completely and totally insane.

"Go on," she said as she gave me another little push.

Here I was, again, in a situation I had no control over; it was beginning to feel like the story of my life! I inched carefully across the floor. My steps were muffled by the thick, ornate carpet on the floor. The clock continued to tick noisily, and for one second I imagined it was the sound of my heart beating — threatening to break right through the wall of my chest.

"Go on, shake him," Christina whispered.

I moved to the side of the chair.

He was stretched out. He was tiny, and his entire body fit neatly into the chair. His hair was white and stuck up in ten thousand different directions. Glasses sat on his nose, and he had a few days' growth of whiskers. He smelled like my grandmother used to smell . . . like that ointment she rubbed all over herself to relieve the pains in her joints.

I bent over closer. I needed to see if he was breathing. I just couldn't tell. I couldn't hear anything except the ticking of the clock. I bent down even closer and put a hand gently against his chest. I looked up and his eyes popped open.

"AAAAAHHHH!" I screamed, stumbling backwards, tripping on a table and tumbling to the floor.

He jumped straight up out of his seat. "What are

you doing, boy? What are you doing in my house?" he yelled.

He stood up, and I was shocked to see he was holding something in his hand, a club or bat. He took a couple of steps toward me. I moved like a crab backwards until I bumped into the wall.

"What do you want? Why are you here?" he yelled. He tottered forward.

"Stop!" Christina yelled. "We just wanted to see if you were okay!"

He stopped and looked over at her. She was backed right up against the wall, and he hadn't seen her before she spoke. I grabbed the wall and pulled myself to my feet. My legs felt all rubbery, and as I tried to retreat a few steps farther I stumbled and almost fell.

"We knocked, and when there wasn't an answer we came in because we were worried something had happened to you," Christina blurted out.

"What?" he asked.

"We knocked and . . ."

"Wait!" he ordered. He fumbled around with something in the front pocket of his shirt. He pulled it out. It looked like a transistor radio with a wire that ran up and into one of his ears. He fiddled with the dials.

"Darn hearing aid," he muttered. "Now, what did you say?"

Christina explained it over again.

"Is that how city kids behave? Bursting into a man's home? A man's home is his castle! I'm sick and tired of hooligans trespassing on my property. This ain't your school."

"We were just worried," she said.

"Worried, hah!" he spat out. "And why were you even here in the first place?"

"We came to ask your help," Christina answered.

"My help?" he asked suspiciously.

"With the whales. We need you help with the whales," I blurted out.

"The whales? What do you mean, boy?"

"There's a pod of pilot whales stranded on the beach on the other side of the island," I explained.

"Whales on the beach? Don't surprise me none, what with that bad storm and all. But why are you troubling an old man about this instead of getting those fancy teachers of yours from the school to take care of it?"

"The fancy teachers . . . I mean Dr. Resney and his wife, had to leave the island because she was having a baby. They got taken out by helicopter last night and nobody has come back to help yet. We can't even call out because the radio is dead," I continued.

"Do you think we could use your radio?" Christina asked.

"Don't have a radio. Sit down and tell me what happened," he said, motioning to the chesterfield.

Christina took a few steps to sit down. I remained frozen to the spot. I didn't want to get any closer. She turned, reached out and grabbed me by the hand. I followed after her. We sat down on an old couch. A puff of dust rose as my bottom hit the cushion.

He moved off to the side and a flash of light appeared in his hand: a match. He protected the flame with his hands and then lit an oil lamp from it. A soft glow filled the room. He hobbled back toward us, leaning heavily on a cane, which my overactive imagination had mistaken for a club when he'd first woken up. He sat back down on the lounger.

"I guess your electricity is still off from the storm," I said, trying to break the silence.

"It's off, but not from the storm. Had them turn it off about ten years ago. Getting too darn expensive. Now, what was it you wanted to know?" he asked.

"We heard you know about whales," Christina answered.

"Some," he countered.

"Pilot whales? About beached pilot whales?" I questioned.

"Seen it seven or eight times in my life."

"Great! Fantastic! What did you do?" Christina exclaimed.

"Killed 'em, of course."

"Killed them! We don't want to kill them, we want to know how to get them back into the water."

"Back in the water? Why would anybody want to do that?" he asked.

"To save them, of course," she replied.

"Save 'em . . . why would I want to do such a darn fool thing?"

"Because they're living creatures," Christina retorted. "Creatures that deserve to live . . . but look who I'm arguing with . . . a man who killed whales for a living."

What was she saying? This was no time to get into

a fight. I edged slightly away from Christina and turned to look at the door leading out.

"That's right. I was a whaler and I'm darn proud of it!"

"It's not right to kill whales."

"But it's all right to kill other things?" he asked.

Boy, I didn't like where that question might be leading.

"Of course it isn't. We shouldn't be killing anything . . ."

"Oh, so is that so, girlie? I guess you must be one of those vegetarian people, huh? Don't eat no fish or chickens or cows or pigs."

Christina paused. She looked sheepish. "Well . . . I do eat some meat."

"Beef? Pork?" he asked.

She nodded her head slightly. "But it's different!"

"Different? How?" he demanded.

"Well . . . whales are free, and cattle are raised to be eaten," she reasoned.

"Seems to me it's worse to raise something its whole life just to be slaughtered. At least the whales were once free and had a chance to stay free," he argued.

"And . . . and whales are smart . . . they're smart animals," she countered.

"Hah! If they're so smart how come they need my help to get off the beach? I never seen a herd of cows stranded before. 'Sides, whales only beach them-selves because something's wrong with 'em. Must be sick or they wouldn't come up on the beach."

"That can't be right," Christina said.

"You come here and tell me I'm an expert and then first thing I say you tell me I'm wrong. Hah!"

Suddenly he started coughing and hacking like he was trying to bring up a hair-ball. He was struggling to catch his breath. He rose to his feet and hobbled out of the room, disappearing from view. The sound of his coughing continued, and then we could hear him spit something up and there was silence. It was obvious we were wasting our time. He wasn't going to help us.

I stood up and grabbed Christina's hand. "Let's get going," I said softly.

She rose to her feet as Mr. Amos re-entered the room.

"Are you okay?" she asked.

"It's nothing . . . nothing at all."

"We have to get going now," I said, edging toward the hallway leading to safety.

"Who's that?" Christina asked unexpectedly, pointing to a picture on the mantel.

What was she doing? This was no time to be taking a tour of the house.

"That's my daughter . . . Christina," he answered.

"That's my name!"

"Is that right? Prettiest name in the world. She was named after my wife."

I knew he lived alone and had to assume his wife had died.

"Does your daughter visit very often?" Christina asked.

He shook his head.

"Does she live far away?" she asked.

"No . . . it isn't that . . . she's . . . gone . . . passed away," he said, his voice barely a whisper.

"That's so sad," Christina said.

"I'm sorry," I mumbled.

He coughed loudly again. "Worst thing about getting old is you outlive the people around you . . . just doesn't seem natural that a man should outlive his daughter . . ."

"Did she have children? Do you have grandchildren?" Christina asked.

"Three. Two boys and a little girl, named Christina." He smiled. "'Course that little girl is now nearly thirty."

"Do you see them very often?"

"Not for years. They write. Christmas cards and stuff."

"Don't they ever call? . . . oh yeah, no phones," I remembered. "We'd better get going."

"To save those whales?" he asked.

"To try," Christina replied.

"How long they been on the beach?"

I wondered why he was asking. "We found them this morning."

"They'll be dead before night. Dry out," Mr. Amos said.

"We're keeping them wet," Christina explained. "That way they won't dry out and the tide will take them back out this evening."

"But we don't know how to get water into them,"

I added. "Do you have any idea how to get them to drink?"

He shrugged his shoulders. "Whales don't drink."

"But everything has to drink," I said.

"Nope. They get their water from their food. There's no place else for them to get water."

"What do you mean? They swim in water."

"Sea water," Mr. Amos said. "Salt water. They can't drink it any more than you can."

I nodded my head. It made sense. There was no more time to discuss anything, though. We had to get out of there. People would start worrying. Ms. Fleming would have a bird if she realized we weren't there. What would she think we were doing?

"Christina we have to get . . ." I stopped. There on the side table was Mike's camera, or more correctly, Mike's dad's camera.

Christina looked at me and I motioned with my eyes. She saw the camera and her eyes widened in surprise.

"Um . . . Mr. Amos . . . um . . . could I take that camera?" Christina asked.

"Camera? You were one of the kids here last night!"

He struggled to his feet and I felt my stomach rise up into my throat.

"Not her. It was me," I said softly, forcing the words out.

"So you thought it would be funny to come on up here and try to scare an old man, did you?"

"We didn't even know you were here. We just

• 171 •

wanted to come up and see the lighthouse," I tried to explain.

"Fine-sounding story!" he snorted.

"Really, it's true. And, I'm sorry."

"Yeah, I bet you are . . . sorry that you dropped it," he said, shaking his head. "Take the camera and get going."

"But —" Christina said.

"Now!" he ordered.

I started for the door.

"We really are sorry, Mr. Amos," Christina said quietly. "It was nice to meet you."

He didn't respond. We walked down the hall and out the door.

We were moving as quickly as we could. I looked at my watch. It was a few minutes before three o'clock, which meant the tide was almost at its lowest level and would soon be rising again. I prayed our absence hadn't been noticed. Hitting the beach, I was amazed at just how far the water had dropped away.

I looked around. Ms. Fleming was nowhere to be seen. Mrs. Murphy was there, busy moving from group to group. I hoped we could slip in without our arrival being noticed, but I wasn't counting on it. After having been in her class a few weeks I was beginning to figure she had eyes in the back of her skull. She didn't miss anything.

Kids were hauling up water, standing and sitting beside the whales. The whales, covered by coloured sheets and blankets, seemed unreal. We headed straight for Captain. Mike was pouring a bucket of

ERIC WALTERS

water on him. His shoulders were stooped and he looked exhausted. I figured that while everybody else had taken breaks or slowed down he had kept moving. I had to admire his determination. Chuckie was nowhere to be seen. Had he gone off to have a break, or was he down by the water refilling the pails?

"How's he doing?" Christina asked.

Mike looked up. "Okay . . . where have you two been?"

"Here's Dad's camera," she said, holding it out as an answer.

"You went to the old man's house?"

"No, we went out and bought a new one," she said sarcastically, handing it to her brother.

"Was it lying by the steps where I dropped it?"

"No, it was in the living room," I replied.

"The living room! You went into the house?"

"Had to. How else could we talk to him?" She made in sound very matter-of-fact, like it was no big deal.

"Why did you want to talk to him?" Mike asked in wide-eyed amazement.

"Mrs. Presley said he knew about whales so we thought he might be able to help us," Christina answered

"And does he? Will he help?"

"Whatever help we get won't be coming from him," I answered. "But he did tell us something. Whales don't drink water. They get it from their food."

"You mean we should be feeding them?"

"I don't think so. They can probably go a day without food . . . I know we could," I said.

Mike nodded. "I hope you're right."

"Wait a second . . . there are more of them . . . more stranded whales," Christina said, changing the subject abruptly.

"Yeah, a lot more," Mike said plaintively. "Twenty-one of them are on the beach, and three more are wallowing in the shallows. If the tide doesn't turn soon they'll be beached too," Mike replied.

"But why are they doing it? Why do they keep coming up onto the beach?" Christina asked.

"I don't know," Mike answered softly. "I just don't know." His voice trailed off. He sounded as tired as he looked.

It didn't make any sense. Why did more and more whales continue to be stranded? It wasn't like with the first few, who'd probably been driven ashore by the waves and winds of the storm. It was like every whale after those first ones was playing some sort of bizarre game of follow-the-leader. Thank goodness they hadn't all decided to play. Dorsal fins and blows regularly broke through the surface of the water of the sheltered little bay. It was hard to tell how many other members of the pod were still hidden beneath the greenish waters, but there were more, many more. Were they all going to end up on the beach?

Chuckie struggled back up the beach carrying a bucket in each hand. He plopped them down heavily on the sand, and water slopped over the edges of both of them.

"Nice of you two to return! Where were you?" he demanded.

Mike held up the camera and Chuckie's eyes bugged out.

"Wow! You went back to the house . . . did you see the ghost?" he asked.

"We met Mr. Amos, the old man who lives there," Christina answered. "Ghosts," she said, shaking her head, "grow up, Chuckie."

"You weren't there last night in the dark," he responded. "But then again, it was even more eerie on the beach here when nobody was around."

"What do you mean?" I asked.

"The whales were talking," Chuckie answered.

"We've heard them talking. So what?" Christina asked.

"Not like this," Chuckie argued. "It was different."

"He's right," Mike agreed. "Maybe we could hear them better because there was nobody around making noise, or maybe they were talking more because they thought they were alone, but it was really something."

"Like from a movie about aliens. I was just glad it wasn't dark."

"Oh, while I'm thinking about it, Ms. Fleming and Mrs. Murphy were asking where the two of you were. I told them you weren't feeling well and you went to lie down," Mike said, motioning to his sister. "And that you were up at the school trying to find more sheets, Gord. So in case she asks you, play along."

"Thanks for covering for . . ." I stopped myself mid-sentence. "But how did you even know you should be giving us an alibi?"

"I didn't. Just force of habit, you know, lying to

teachers. I figured whatever you were doing was your own business."

I nodded. "I see Mrs. Murphy. Is Ms. Fleming up at the school looking for me?" I asked in alarm.

"No, she's down here," Chuckie replied.

"I don't see her," Christina noted.

"You wouldn't. She's out there," Mike said, pointing out to the inlet. "She's scuba diving."

"Out there with all the whales?"

"That would be amazing!" Christina said. "Just amazing!"

I couldn't imagine going out there. There was no telling how many whales were thrashing around out there, but what was certain was that they were all much bigger than any of us and they probably weren't too happy.

"Chuckie, you and Christina go and fill some more buckets. Gord, help me pour these on Captain," Mike directed.

Chuckie sighed deeply. He looked bone tired.

"Come on," Christina said as she handed him two empty buckets. They headed down to the water. As Mike poured the first bucket I grabbed another and handed it to him.

"You two were just talking to that old man, right?" Mike asked.

"Yeah. Why?" I asked apprehensively.

"It's just I heard some talk."

"What kind of talk," I asked, feigning innocence.

He finished with the second bucket, turned and moved up close to me. Mike was a lot bigger than me and I had to tip my head back to look up at him.

"Stupid talk. Talk I didn't like. She's my baby sister and nobody bothers her in any way. Understand?"

"Yeah, I understand. We're just friends, honestly."

"Good. It would be a shame," Mike stated.

"What would be a shame?" I asked, although I really didn't want to know the answer to my question.

"It would be a shame to have to rearrange your face. I was just starting to like you . . . well, at least like you a little."

"Um . . . thanks, I guess," I stammered in response.

"Taking away my best friend is bad enough, but I can live with that."

"I'm not taking your best friend!" I objected. "I was hoping . . . hoping . . . we could all be friends."

Mike nodded his head slowly and his scowl dissolved slightly. "Maybe. Maybe you can come over to my house sometime." He shoved a bucket into my stomach. "Quit talking and get working. More water."

3:45 P.M.

"Look, the flag is in the water!" somebody shouted.

A ripple of electricity surged along the beach as all eyes turned toward the tall wooden stake with the sock tied to the top. It had been moved every half hour to mark the level of the water. For the past six hours the water had repeatedly retreated from the flag, leaving it high and dry. Now for the first time it was submerged. The tide was coming back in! The tide was turning! I had to laugh . . . I remembered hearing my mother use that term before when something was changing for the better, but I never thought it would actually happen.

I started to run down to the water's edge. It was like the tiredness had instantly drained out of my legs. I sprinted, feeling so elated that it was like my feet were hardly touching the sand as I moved.

The last three of the whales, bringing the total to twenty-four, had been stranded only barely out of the water. Already the waves were starting to break over their tails. All three were among the smaller whales. I took a slight detour over to where they lay. I put down one of the buckets and reached out to touch the closest of the whales. Its skin was still rubbery, and in response to my touch it started to move its flippers and tail frantically. If the tide came in as fast as it left then these three wouldn't be out of the water any more than an hour.

"Don't worry, guys. It won't be long," I said softly.

I looked up in time to catch sight of Ms. Fleming coming out of the water. Kids were already starting to cluster around her, and Mrs. Murphy came over to her side. I wanted to hear what she had seen, but it was best not to approach her right now. The more time that passed the less chance she'd remember to ask where Christina and I had been.

As I started to walk back up the beach with my buckets full, Mrs. Murphy called everybody over. As we assembled I could feel the charge in the air. The rising water had washed away the sense of despair and hopelessness that seemed to be gripping everybody. I knew we were all tired, some near exhaustion, but the end was within sight.

"For those who I didn't tell already, it was fascinating out there!" Ms. Fleming said to anybody who would listen. Her swim mask sat on the top of her head and the tanks were sitting on the sand by her feet.

"How many whales are out there?" Mike asked.

"I really couldn't tell for sure. The visibility is pretty limited. But I must have been buzzed or had close contact with a dozen or more whales. It was just incredible! But I'll tell everybody about it later. First, we have some things to discuss."

"Yes we do," Mrs. Murphy said. "As we all know, the tide is coming back in."

A cheer went up from the gathering and kids exchanged smiles, back slaps and high-fives, like they were somehow responsible for the returning water.

"We have to keep on working. High tide is five hours away, and by then most of the whales will be free."

Again a burst of cheers came forth. Wait a second . . . what did she mean *most* of the whales? Why not all of them? I turned and looked up and away from the crowd. Captain was far from the water's edge. The sheets were glistening in the sun.

"Captain's big and strong. He'll be fine," Christina said, leaning over and whispering in my ear.

I was starting to get spooked by her putting my thoughts into words. But while she was right about what I was thinking, she was wrong about Captain. He was big, but I didn't think he was strong any more. His breathing had become even more irregular, with longer periods between breaths. When Christina was down at the water the last time I'd peeled away part of one of the sheets covering him. His skin looked dull and lifeless. I'd put the sheet back down before she could see it.

"We're all going to work with the whales closest to the water. We have to work together. Once those first few whales swim free we'll move to the next group."

"We're not giving up on Captain!" Christina objected, taking to her feet.

"We're not giving up on anybody," Ms. Fleming answered. "After we've freed a whale, there'll be time for groups to go back and work with their own whale before the water reaches the next whale at the shoreline."

"Okay," Christina agreed, sitting back down beside me.

"And by the way, are you feeling better?" Ms. Fleming asked her.

"Yeah, much better, for sure."

"And you, Gordon. Did you find what you were looking for?"

"Yes, ma'am," I answered.

There was a twittering of voices and giggling all around us. I looked down at my crossed legs.

"The waves are getting a little bit rough. Please be careful when you get into the water. Stay close to your buddy and *please* don't take any chances," Mrs. Murphy said.

4:06 P.M.

Most of the boys had stripped out of their T-shirts, and of course, our shoes and socks had been abandoned long before. The waves were crashing down with more force and the wind whipped up salty spray. I was feeling cold.

Ten of us lined up against the first whale — five on one side by the tail and five on the other side by the head. Mike, Chuckie and I were by the head, and the water was only halfway up our thighs. Those by the tail were submerged over their waists. The water was now deep enough that the whale was rising up with each wave, and I estimated that more than half of it was floating.

"Okay, everybody get ready! We'll push when the next wave comes," Ms. Fleming commanded.

We were going to try to turn the whale around. We had to point it back to open water.

"Ready . . ."

I placed my hands gently against the creature's side. The skin felt cold and rubbery and smooth.

"Now!"

I braced my legs and pushed with all my might. A wave surged in and I felt myself being lifted up. I struggled to keep my feet on the bottom and pushed with all my might. The wave crashed up on the beach.

"That's it!" Ms. Fleming cheered. "We're doing it! Get ready for the next wave!"

I looked up and realized she was right, we had

made some progress. The whale had been turned ever so slightly, but in the right direction.

"Get ready again! A big one is getting ready to break!" Ms. Fleming yelled.

"Now! Push now!"

I pressed hard. The wave broke over top of my head, but I kept on pushing hard. I felt the whale move. The wave receded.

"Wonderful! Wonderful!" Ms. Fleming yelled. Kids were cheering.

I wiped the stinging salt water away from my eyes. The whale was now turned almost perpendicular to the shore. The next wave broke before anybody could say anything, and the whale rose up and then washed slightly back out. Its fins started to move furiously and it raised its tail and then slammed it back down into the water, throwing water high into the air. Kids scrambled out of the way. Everybody else had stopped working and formed a semicircle on the beach, watching. Two more waves broke and the whale continued to struggle but wasn't able to free itself.

"All of you on this side!" Ms. Fleming ordered. "We have to push it into deeper water!"

I took a place midway along the whale. It was crowded as many more than the ten of us took positions. The extra hands could only help.

"This time hold firm when the wave hits and then push when it starts to wash back out," Ms. Fleming yelled. "Dig in your feet . . . get ready . . . it's coming."

The wave rushed in and the whale was pushed toward us. I had a rush of fear. What would happen if somehow I was sucked underneath the whale and trapped? I pressed against it with all my strength, straining to hold it in place, suspended on the wave. Just as I thought I couldn't hold on any longer the wave started out again and I pressed with all my might. I could feel it moving away, out to deeper water.

"Push! Push! Push!" Ms. Fleming screamed. "Push! It's moving! Push!"

I put one foot forward and then another. We were doing it. All at once something smashed against my legs and I was swept off my feet. My head plunged beneath the water. My feet touched bottom and I pushed off to pop up out of the water. Everybody was cheering wildly. I shook my head to clear the water away from my face.

The whale was about three metres away. It exhaled loudly through its blowhole and its fins broke the surface. One of those fins must have been what had knocked me off my feet. The whale was swimming freely. It was parallelling the shore. It dipped down and the dorsal fin partially buried itself beneath the waves. It was beautiful, just plain beautiful. I walked out of the waves.

"We did it," I said out loud, more to myself than to anybody else.

"What is that whale doing?" I heard a voice call out.

The whale had turned back around and was once again headed toward the land. Kids screamed and yelled. Mike ran into the waves, directly at the whale, like he was going to try to stop it. The whale ploughed forward, driven by its massive tail, brushing aside

Mike and continuing up to the shore. It surfed up until it was once again solidly beached.

I felt numb all over. How could this happen? People stood in stunned silence. From behind me I heard sobbing. It was Christina. She was sitting on the sand with her knees up and her head buried in her arms. More sobbing. She wasn't the only one in tears.

There was one other sound; the whale was talking, and its voice was being answered. The whales were calling out at a frantic pace.

"I don't know what more we can do," Ms. Fleming said forlornly. "I just don't know."

I turned away and looked for Mike. Maybe he had an answer. He was farther up the beach, alone, walking away. I trotted up beside him.

"What are we going to do, Mike?"

He didn't answer.

"Mike?" He still didn't answer. "Mike?" I placed a hand on his shoulder. "Mike . . ."

"Leave me alone!" he said angrily, turning back to face me. "I don't know what to do!" He brushed his hand across his eyes. He was trying to clear away the tears.

"We have to be able to do something," I argued.

"Nothing. There's nothing to do without help. We need somebody to tell us what to do."

"But Mike, we can still —"

"Go away, I want to be alone for a minute."

I wanted to say something else, but instead I took a few steps back toward the others. Then I saw a boat enter the bay and my heart skipped a beat.

"Mike, look! Look!" I shouted "It's a boat!"

Mike was almost instantly at my shoulder. "Where is it?" he asked. "There it is! Come on!" he said, answering his own question.

We ran up the beach to join the others. They'd also noticed the incoming boat.

"Is it Dr. Resney?" I heard Chuckie ask.

"It's got to be," Ms. Fleming replied. "Or somebody he sent."

"No, it isn't," I disagreed.

"How do you know?" Ms. Fleming asked. Others shot me questioning looks.

"He knows," Christina said. "It's Mr. Amos."

"From the story?" Jenna asked in disbelief.

"No, from the island. We were talking to him and asked him for his help," Christina replied.

"When were you two . . . ?" Ms. Fleming let the sentence trail off. "The three of us have to talk . . . but not now."

Mr. Amos was sitting in the stern of the open boat. Its engine chugged away, sending up a thin cloud of blue smoke. He was headed straight for us. He killed the engine as he closed in on the shore and tilted the motor up out of the water. The boat continued to move forward, pushed ahead with each wave.

"Help him get ashore," Mrs. Murphy ordered.

Christina and I, along with Mike, Chuckie and a couple of others, waded into the surf. Mr. Amos stood up in the boat and heaved a rope toward us. It landed in the water. Mike picked it up and started to reel it in. The rest of us helped. We pulled the bow of the boat up onto the beach. Mr. Amos jumped out into the shallow water. Over his shoulder was a large duffel bag.

"Didn't expect to see me, did you?" he said to me. He was right about that.

"Thanks for coming, Mr. Amos!" Christina beamed.

"Don't thank me yet."

Ms. Fleming and Mrs. Murphy rushed over and introduced themselves.

"You look like a teacher," he said to Mrs. Murphy. "But, shoot, you're hardly old enough to be out of school yourself," he said to Ms. Fleming. He paused. "I recognize you two," he said, pointing toward Mike and Chuckie. I had to admit, it would have been hard to forget Mike's shaved head and Chuckie's green hair.

"You do?" Ms. Fleming asked. "From when?"

"Last night, around two in the morning. Aren't you supposed to make sure they don't come wandering around in the middle of the night?"

"Yes, I am," Mrs. Murphy replied. She turned and glared at the two of them.

"Can you help?" Christina asked.

Mr. Amos didn't answer. "There's more whales here than you said. A lot more."

"They keep on beaching themselves," Mike noted.

"Got to look at 'em," Mr. Amos replied.

"I'll show you," Christina offered.

He nodded his head. "Bring your friend along too," he said, pointing at me.

He started to walk away and then turned back to the teachers. "Have the rest of 'em stop . . . get some food and rest . . . no sense doing anything till the tide is higher."

"I'm staying here!" Mike said defiantly.

Mr. Amos fixed him with an angry stare. "He don't listen too good does he?"

"Not too well," Ms. Fleming agreed.

"He better learn to listen. I seen enough of that boy last night. Either he does what he's told or I'm not doing nothing," Mr. Amos announced.

Mike planted his feet in the sand and folded his arms across his chest. He didn't look like he was going anywhere. Christina walked over to Mike and said something. He nodded his head and started to walk away, toward the school. Whatever she'd said had obviously worked. In one way, I was surprised that Mike had listened, but then I thought about who he was listening to. Maybe she was younger than him, and the same age as the rest of us, but she seemed older, more mature, than any twelve-year-old I'd ever met.

As everybody else walked off in the other direction, we trailed behind Mr. Amos. In one hand he held a cane. Over the other shoulder was the duffel bag. We came to the first whale. He circled around it slowly, reaching down and touching it with his hand a few times, muttering to himself.

"How much you figure this fella weighs?" he asked.

"I don't know . . . seven or eight hundred kilograms," I guessed.

"No more than five hundred . . . this one is no more than two or three years old . . . female."

I was impressed. He did know his whales.

"Probably get about two hundred kilograms of blubber, that would render down to three or four barrels of oil."

Christina looked at me in shock. "What are you talking about?"

"Just thinking out loud," he answered.

"Is the whale going to be okay?" I asked, changing the subject.

"Hard to tell. Never tried to put one back in the water. Skin is good, colour isn't bad." He looked up at me. "They get more black the longer they're out of the water. I think this one might make it."

The whale took a deep breath and somewhere along the beach another whale exhaled loudly. It was then that I noticed how quiet it was. The rest of the kids had retreated well up the beach, led by Ms. Fleming and Mrs. Murphy. As I watched, they disappeared around the point. All that remained were the whales, Mr. Amos, Christina, and me. Mr. Amos was off toward the next whale.

"I don't trust him," Christina said under her breath.

I didn't know what to say.

"I'm going to keep my eye on him," she continued.

We rushed over to his side, beside the next whale.

"Hear that?" Mr. Amos asked.

I perked up my ears. "The whales are talking."

"Yep, singing their songs. Sound we used to listen to when we were hunting 'em. Music to the ears of a whaler."

He stood up and moved to the next whale. He went through the same routine; circling around, touching, peeling back the sheets or covers, poking and muttering to himself. He was moving his way up the beach, going from whale to whale, from those closest to the water to those farthest away.

"What are you doing?" Christina asked suspiciously.

"Trying to figure out which ones are a waste of time."

"What do you mean?"

"Meant what I said," Mr. Amos said. He limped away up the incline toward Captain.

"What did he mean?" Christina asked when he was safely out of hearing range.

"I don't know," I answered honestly. "Like you said, let's stay close and watch. By the way, what did you say to Mike?"

"Not much," she answered.

"It had to be something. It got him to move pretty quick," I reasoned.

"I just told him he was being a jerk and that you and I would take care of things. Mike is really pretty easy to get along with."

Yeah, right, I thought.

Mr. Amos was slowly circling around Captain. We watched him in silence.

"You know who this fella is?" he asked.

"We call him Captain," Christina replied.

"Captain?"

"We named him. We named all of them," she explained.

"Never heard of such foolishness. This isn't a pet

. . . though you have the right idea. This is the largest male. He is like the captain of this pod."

He peeled back the sheets. Captain's skin was jet black, and looked even worse than when I'd looked at it earlier. I realized part of the skin had come off on the sheets. He lay the sheet back down and then went and crouched down by the whale's head. Captain's eyes were closed. Just as I wondered if he was already dead, the massive back rose slightly as he took a breath.

He leaned over and placed a hand on the whale. He seemed to be talking to it, although I couldn't make out any of the words. Then he turned to where we stood.

"All these whales . . . on the beach and in the bay . . . this is the leader. He's the granddaddy of 'em all."

"All of them? The whole pod?" I asked in disbelief.

"Yep, all of 'em. A pod is just another name for a family. Whales are born, live and die with their families. That's the way it is with pilot whales."

With some difficulty he struggled to his feet. "You two go and join your friends. Get some food, and rest, and be back here in another hour or so."

"What are you going to be doing?" Christina questioned.

"Lots of things," he answered.

"Like what?"

"For one thing, trying to find the biggest male closest to the water."

"How can you tell male from female?" Christina asked.

"If it's real big it's going to be a male. Then to be

sure you look at the dorsal fin. Female's is straight and the male's curves under. But this ain't no science class, go on now," he said, shooing us away.

We started walking. I knew that Christina didn't ask how Captain was doing because she was afraid of the answer.

"He said he was going to do lots of things but he only mentioned one," Christina noted. "What else is he going to do?"

"I don't know."

"I don't trust him," she said. "Do you?"

"Didn't you just ask me that?"

"You didn't answer me," she said, with a questioning look.

"What choice do we have?"

As we reached the point I looked over my shoulder. Mr. Amos was fumbling around with something in his duffel bag. He pulled out a long metal object. It looked like . . . like a shotgun! I stopped and spun around completely.

"What's wrong?"

My answer was drowned out by the explosion of the gun.

I reeled back in shock.

"What is he . . . ?" Christina started to ask before her words were stopped by a second blast of the shotgun.

The gun was aimed at Captain's head, and even from a distance I could see the whale "shrug" as the impact hit, while Mr. Amos was simultaneously thrown slightly backwards by the recoil of the weapon. He took the sheet and pulled it up so that it covered the whale's head.

There was total silence. Even the wind and waves seemed to have been silenced, as if waiting for what was to come next.

"Murderer!" Christina screamed. "Murderer!" She brushed past me and started running for him.

Her reaction caught me almost as much by surprise as what had just happened. My brain unfroze, and before it had a chance to think how stupid it was, I raced after her.

"Murderer! You're nothing but a stinking whale killer!" she shrieked.

She was running like the wind and I stumbled a couple of times in my dash to catch her. She was almost at him; only a small slice of beach and the corpse of Captain stood between her and Mr. Amos. In a burst of speed I caught up and wrapped my arms around her from behind. She struggled to get away and then stopped, turned around and threw her arms around me. She burst into tears and I could feel the deep sobs in her chest vibrate into mine.

I felt a flush go through my entire body. I didn't know which was more disturbing, what had just happened to Captain or what was taking place right now. I patted her on the back, the way my mother would try and comfort me when I was little and had fallen down and hurt myself. I looked up and saw Mr. Amos studying us.

"Why? Why did you kill him?" I asked.

Christina released her grip on me and turned to face Mr. Amos. She wiped her eyes with her hand.

"Why did you do it?" I asked again.

"Told you two to go up and join the others. Told you I had things to do . . . things I didn't think you should be watching."

"You killed him! You killed him!" she sobbed.

Mr. Amos put the shotgun down on the ground on top of the bag. He made a gagging, hacking sound and then spat onto the ground.

"Go on now, back up to the school, and let me finish what has to be done," he said.

"Finish it? You want us gone so nobody sees you murder these creatures. You're a murderer!" Christina spat at him.

"Killing him was the kindest thing I could've done."

"How can you say such a thing? We were saving him!" she protested angrily.

"Nope. All you were doing was stopping him from dying. That's a whole different thing. Poor old whale was worse than dead . . . suffering and in pain with no hope. Had to stop the pain."

"What do you mean, 'poor old whale,' like you really care about a whale or whether it's in pain. You're a whaler!"

"That's God's truth, and I'm proud of what I did."

"Proud of killing helpless whales?" It was obvious that Christina couldn't believe what she was hearing.

"Proud of feeding my family, and working the seas and surviving. Just 'cause I killed 'em don't mean I don't respect 'em . . . like I respect all life."

"As if I'm supposed to believe you," she said defiantly.

He coughed again, and his whole frame was wracked by the action. "You wanna keep on disrespecting me or do you want me to explain this to you?"

Christina looked at me for an answer. I nodded my head.

"Firstly, that whale was at death's door. You were trying to save him, but you couldn't . . . all you were doing was making the death slower and more painful."

"He was going downhill," I acknowledged.

"It was an old whale. Probably sick or even dying before any of this happened. A healthy whale doesn't get tossed up on the beach like that."

"But all these whales are up on the beach," I said.

"Yep, but that's different. They beached themselves, most pointing straight toward land. Look at this one . . . he's sideways. He was tossed up."

"But weren't they all thrown up by the storm?" Christina asked.

"No," I responded, answering for him. "Only a few. Remember, there were only seven of them here this morning. It was like the rest of them, I don't know, wanted to join the ones that were already on the beach."

"That's right!" Mr. Amos cackled. "That's right. They're all family. The ones in the water were trying to join the ones on the beach."

"Were they were being drawn up by the singing?" Christina asked quietly.

Mr. Amos nodded. "And as long as that old fella, their leader, was singing, they'd keep trying to come to his side."

"You mean they deliberately beached themselves to try and join their leader?" I asked in amazement.

"That doesn't make sense," Christina disagreed.

"Wanting to be with your family and risking your life to do it doesn't make sense to you?" he asked.

I felt his words like a punch in the stomach.

"It just seems hard to believe —" Christina started to say.

"He's right," I interrupted. "I know he's right."

"Course I'm right. Some types of whales are funny like that. Pilot whales maybe more than any others."

"What do we do now?" Christina asked.

"We ain't doing nothing. You two are going up to the school . . . like I already told you to do . . . and I'm going to finish things here."

"What sort of things?" she asked.

"I'm going to mark the high-water line, for one thing," Mr. Amos said.

"And?" she asked.

"And I'm going to deal with the ones that can't live . . . too sick, lungs filled up with liquid, too far above the high-water mark to make it back into the water."

"How many?" I asked. "How many have to . . . ?"

"Three . . . maybe four . . . maybe five."

"You're going to . . ." Christina's words trailed off.

He nodded his head in acknowledgment. "Go on up to the school."

"No," Christina said with quiet determination.

Mr. Amos's brow furrowed in disapproval

"He's got to do it," I said.

"I know," she practically whispered, "but I'm not leaving."

"But we don't want to stay. He's going to have to . . ."

"Kill them," she said, finishing my sentence, one of us finally saying the words. "I can't just walk away."

I looked up at Mr. Amos. "We're staying."

Mr. Amos hammered a series of wooden pegs into the sand to mark the line where the tide would stop rising. At first I questioned in my mind how he could be so certain about where he placed the markers, but he said he knew. Somehow I found his certainty comforting; after all, it was good to have somebody know what was happening.

Three whales were at least partially above this line. For the rest, the water would eventually come up and meet them. Already five whales had been re-submerged. Two had used the rising waters to wiggle back out and return to the open waters. For the other three, we'd watched first with hope and then bitter disappointment. Rather than returning to the water they had simply propelled themselves farther up the beach, so they were no closer to freedom than they were before.

"But if Captain's gone, why are they still trying to come up to the land?" Christina cried out.

"'Cause of that fella there," Mr. Amos said, pointing to a large whale. "I figure he's now the leader."

"What do you mean?" I asked.

"Biggest male takes over the leadership of the pod. That's the way it happens."

"Does that mean you have to . . . have to . . . ?" Christina asked, letting the question trail off.

"Nope. He's healthy and close enough to the water to get back in. We start with him when the time comes."

Finally Mr. Amos pulled out his shotgun again.

With each of the whales, and in the end it was four more, he took great pains to explain to us why he had no choice: two were in bad shape, drying up and near death; one was just too far above the high-water mark; and the fourth had an unexplained series of wounds along its side which had become infected and festered. He thought the wounds might have been from a shark or killer whale attack.

Each time, before he fired, he had us retreat up the beach behind him, away from the line of fire and the sight of the impact. Christina turned around and looked in the other direction, while I simply lowered my eyes to the ground.

For me it was like passing a horrible traffic accident; I didn't want to look but I just had to. The last time he was going to shoot I raised my eyes and watched as the blast tore into the side of the whale's head. With a sickening rush I feared I was going to vomit, instead swallowed hard, took a deep breath, and realized with relief that I'd be okay. He covered up the wound, as well as the entire head, with a sheet, declaring the whale dead, as he had with the other four.

Mr. Amos broke open the gun one last time and let the two spent cartridges drop to the ground. He placed the gun back into his duffel bag. I walked over and stood beside him.

"What now?" I asked.

"I'm gonna sit down here and rest my old bones."

"And us?"

"You two are going up to the school. Eat, rest, explain to the rest of them what I had to do, and then come on back down here."

"How soon do you want us back?" I asked.

He turned over his wrist and looked at his watch. "Forty-five minutes or so."

"Isn't there anything we can do here, now?" Christina asked.

"Nothing nobody can do. We're just waiting for the tide to come back. I'll be waiting, listening, planning."

"We should stay here," Christina objected.

"Nope. Nothing here for you to do, and I need you both with food in your stomachs and strength in your limbs. When the time comes, you both have important things I'll need you to do."

"What? What are we going to be doing?" I asked anxiously.

He didn't answer.

"Before we go, can I ask you a question?" Christina said.

"Question? Sure you can ask . . . don't know if I'll answer it though."

"When my brother and Chuckie and Gord came to your house last night —"

"Which one of them is your brother?" Mr. Amos interrupted. "The one with the funny hair or no hair?"

"The bald one. He shaves his head."

"Hmmph! Imagine such foolishness. Wait till he gets to be half my age and he'll pray to have hair atop his head."

"Maybe," Christina said. "But when they came, were you really firing your gun at them?"

"Firing at them?" he asked in amazement. "Where

would you get such a silly idea?"

Christina looked at me.

"When we were running away we heard a gunshot."

He started to laugh. "That was no gunshot. It was this," he said, holding up his cane. "I smashed it down against the railing to scare you off." A smile came to his face. "And it seemed to work right good."

Christina started to laugh, and I couldn't help but smile myself.

"Now, can I ask you a question?" He turned to me.

"Okay," I answered, nervously.

"Were you three really just coming to take some pictures?"

"That's all, honestly. We just wanted to come and take some pictures to prove to everybody that we'd been right there at the lighthouse . . . you know, to show that we weren't afraid of Captain Amos's ghost."

"Captain Amos?"

"Well . . . this is embarrassing," I stammered. "I know it's just a story Dr. Resney made up to scare us, but we wanted to show everybody."

"He told you a story about Captain Amos, did he?"

"I don't think he meant any offence, naming the character after you," Christina interjected.

"I'm not offended," Mr. Amos replied. "'Sides, he wasn't talking about me. I think he was telling about my great-great-uncle. Leastways, if he was talking about how Captain Amos went mad and killed three people with an axe."

"You mean . . . ?"

He nodded his head. "Ain't no made-up story."

6:15 P.M.

We got back to the school and found Ms. Fleming and Mrs. Murphy talking with a group of girls at the front of the dining hall. Christina and I had talked about it on the walk up from the beach and agreed we'd tell our teachers and let them tell everybody else.

"How are things going on the beach?" Mrs. Murphy asked.

"Um . . . okay . . . can we talk to you two?" I stammered.

"Alone," Christina added.

Mrs. Murphy and Ms. Fleming exchanged a look of concern.

"Excuse us, girls," Mrs. Murphy said. "Come this way."

Mrs. Murphy pushed through the swinging door leading into the kitchen. She held it open for Ms. Fleming, Christina, and me. Mrs. Presley was at the counter making sandwiches. She turned around at our entrance.

"Couldn't believe it when I heard it. How did you two talk him into helping?"

"We were as surprised as anybody when he showed up," I admitted.

"What did you want to tell us?" Ms. Fleming asked. There was more than a hint of anxiousness to her voice.

"Five of the whales aren't alive any more," Christina replied.

"That's sad, but to be expected," Mrs. Murphy said.

"No, you don't understand . . . Mr. Amos killed them."

"He did what?" Mrs. Murphy asked in shock.

"He shot them," I said. It sounded even more dramatic than I thought it would, like a line out of a movie or something.

"My good Lord, why would he do such a monstrous thing?" Ms. Fleming demanded.

"He did it because he had to," I started to explain.

"He had no right to kill those whales. No right whatsoever! We have to get to the beach immediately before he kills any more whales!"

"No, he won't! You have to trust him. He knows what he's doing, honestly!" Christina said.

"You have no idea what he might do! You just met the man!"

"But I didn't!" Mrs. Presley interrupted. "I've know that man since I was old enough to remember."

We all turned to face her.

"And he's stubborn, bad tempered, would argue with a fencepost if it would answer him back . . . and honest. If he came to help then that's what he's doing. If he said he had to kill those whales, then he had to do it. Period, end of discussion! And if you two ladies want to argue any more you'll be fixing your own sandwiches!"

They both looked to the ground. They reminded me of two small children who'd been scolded by their teacher instead of two teachers.

"Let me explain things," I said, "and then you can explain it to everybody else."

Ms. Fleming looked shaken as I relayed the story to her. Mrs. Murphy put an arm around her shoulder.

"I want the two of you to go out and get some food, and get into dry clothing if you have any left," Mrs. Murphy directed.

We started for the door to the dining room.

"And Christina and Gordon," she called out.

We stopped and turned.

"I don't want you to talk to anybody about this right now."

We both nodded and continued out through the door.

6:55 P.M.

Mrs. Murphy had us all gather together one more time. There was a sense of quiet determination throughout the room.

"I want to start by saying that Christina and Gord have brought us news."

The crowd bubbled with conversation as speculation and questions spun around the room. Mrs. Murphy raised her hand above her head and the talking stopped.

"Two whales have freed themselves," she began.

The room erupted into cheers and howls. Once again she raised her hand and the noise level fell.

"But I am sad to tell you that five whales have died."

Suddenly the room was silent. I looked around at the people sitting close to me and could see the expressions of sadness and shock. I was sure everybody was wondering if it was their whale. At least I didn't have to wonder. Poor old Captain.

"It was to be expected. Out of respect, the whales have been completely covered in sheets. Please leave them alone."

Mrs. Murphy and Ms. Fleming had decided, for now at least, against telling the kids how the whales had died. That left a secret shared only by a few of us, including Mike. Christina had insisted that we tell him, and I didn't want to argue with either of them, although I was beginning to realize she was the tougher of the two. We'd had to track him down, but we'd finally found him curled up in a ball in our room. At first he'd been enraged that Mr. Amos had killed the whales. It wasn't easy to calm him down, but finally, after the anger passed, he understood. Mike agreed not to talk to anybody about it.

"We have to work together, and work hard, until the tide rises. How long is that from now?" Mrs. Murphy asked Ms. Fleming.

"Slightly more than two hours."

"Thank you. In just over two hours we will have to put those whales back in the water."

"And if we can't?" a voice called from the back.

"We can," Mrs. Murphy answered quietly. "We can."

7:30 P.M.

"I want all of you to shut up and come here. I'm going to be telling you what you need to be doing!" Mr. Amos shouted.

Instantly everybody gathered around. Those closest settled to the ground, allowing the kids behind to see him.

I looked beyond everybody to the water's edge. A dozen whales were scattered on the beach above the water line. Half a dozen others were now on the line between beach and ocean. Farther out, hidden beneath the water, were possibly dozens and dozens of other whales, the brothers and sisters and countless other relatives of the ones on the beach. I wondered how they felt, separated from their family, so close but not able to help.

I heard an explosion of breath and a saw a dorsal fin skimming the surface. Farther out there were two large heads, side by side, spy-hopping, trying to see onto the beach.

"Gordon?"

I'd been lost in thought, and at the mention of my name I startled and looked at Mr. Amos.

"Do you think you and Christina can handle that job?" he asked.

"Um . . . yeah, sure," I answered, not knowing what he meant, but too unnerved to say anything.

"And I need two more to come out with me in the boat. They need to be good swimmers and strong."

There was a rumbling of response and Mike's name was voiced and fingers pointed toward him. Nobody was as strong as him.

"I can do it," Mike volunteered, rising from the sand.

"You?" Mr. Amos questioned sternly. His expression

softened. "Why not? It's like we're old friends, ain't it? Might as well bring along your buddy . . . the one who looks like a big stock of broccoli."

"Cool!" Chuckie said, jumping to his feet.

"And what do you want the rest of us to do?" Ms. Fleming asked.

"You stay close to Gordon and Christina. They have the most important job. The rest need to keep pouring water on the animals for now. But get ready to help when we call for you. We'll need everybody's strong backs."

The crowd dispersed, leaving the four of us and Ms. Fleming standing around Mr. Amos.

"You two go and get the boat in the water," he said to Mike and Chuckie. "Point it out to open water and wait for me."

They quickly left.

"Come," he directed.

The three of us trailed behind him. He had a coil of rope slung over one of his shoulders. He stopped at the tail of the largest remaining whale. The rising tide had brought it much closer to the water but it was still completely on the sand.

"Pull those sheets off the beast," he commanded.

Ms. Fleming followed his order. She started to ball them up when he took one and wrapped it loosely around the whale's tail.

"This should stop the rope from digging in too deep."

He took the rope in his hand and forced it between the whale's tail and the sand, circling it all the way around. The tail was practically as thick as his arms were wide. He pulled the end of the rope until he had a long section, perhaps four or five metres, on the far side of the whale.

"Here's where you all gotta watch real good," he explained.

The three of us bent in close.

"This is a special type of knot."

His hands worked to weave the long end of the rope around in a series of loops. He pulled it snugly around the tail. The whale remained immobile and impassive, as if it weren't even aware we were there.

"Finished. This here end will be run out to the boat. The harder it gets tugged the tighter it gets. Give it a pull," he directed.

I took the end from him and pulled, at first gently and then putting all my weight behind it. It became taut.

"Now, I want you to keep pulling, hard . . . and I want you to take this end and give it a little tug," he said, handing the other end to Christina.

She took the rope and pulled on it. Instantly I tumbled backwards onto the sand. I picked myself up.

"Simple as that is how she works. One end is for pulling and the other end is for releasing. Here, let me show you all again and then I want to see you do it right a few times."

This time we all watched intently as Mr. Amos showed us how to tie the knot. I had trouble following it, as did Ms. Fleming, but Christina caught on quickly. He seemed frustrated by our lack of ability, but Christina was able to explain and demonstrate it in a way that we both were able to understand.

"And remember, it's important you tie this knot the right way. It has to release," he warned us.

"It couldn't live with all that rope attached, could it?" Christina asked.

"Maybe, maybe not, but it ain't the whale you should be worried for."

"What do you mean?" Ms. Fleming asked.

"The other end of the rope is tied to my boat. If the whale dived before we were able to cut the rope it could flip us right over."

Ms. Fleming's expression reflected the fear I felt.

"'Course that shouldn't happen. The two boys with me will be keeping the rope free of the engine and cutting us free if need be . . . leastways that's what I hope."

Christina looped the rope over the tail again, setting the knot in place. She looked up at Mr. Amos and he answered with a smile.

"I'm going to the boat. We'll position it in as close as we can and then Gordon you have to wade out and throw us the rope. Okay?"

I nodded.

"And once the rope is in place I need every kid to take a place on the line or get ready to push the whale from the side. This boat doesn't have much power so we need everybody to help. Everybody understand?"

"Well, yes, but I was just wondering. Shouldn't we be starting with one of the smaller whales, closer to the water?" Ms. Fleming questioned. "Wouldn't that make more sense?"

Mr. Amos shook his head. "I ain't got time for this. You two explain it to her." He walked away to the boat. Ms. Fleming turned to us.

"We have to release the biggest male first," Christina explained.

"Once he's back in the water the others won't be fighting us to stay on the beach. They'll want to get into the water to join him," I continued.

"Are you sure about this?" Ms. Fleming asked, sounding concerned.

"Positive," I answered. Christina nodded in agreement.

"But how can you tell this is a male?"

"By the dorsal fin," I replied.

"Yeah, look here," Christina said, touching it by the fin. "See the way it curves under? With a female it's more pointy and straight."

"Mr. Amos explained it all to us," I offered in explanation.

Our discussion was stopped by the sound of an air horn. I looked up to see Mr. Amos, along with Mike and Chuckie, on the boat, waving and waiting for the rope. I took a deep breath. It was time.

The coil of rope was strung over my shoulder. I let it out carefully as I waded into the water. To have any chance of throwing it to them, I'd have to get pretty close to the boat. The slope was gradual and fairly smooth, with only an occasional pothole. This made it easier to walk along the bottom, but it also meant I had to go a long way out. It might get deep, or at least deeper than I had been before when I was just splashing around right near the shore. I thought about the whales gliding around under the surface of the waters, hidden from my view, and wondered what else could be under there, out of sight.

I felt a tug on the rope and looked back to see that kids were already taking up places on the line, getting ready to pull. I stumbled forward at the same time a wave broke, and for a split second I sank below the surface. Desperately I planted my feet and pushed above the surface.

The boat was only a dozen metres in front of me, bobbing up and down on the waves. The engine hummed gently, releasing a thin line of bluish smoke, which drifted up into the sky.

"Throw it!" Mike yelled. "Throw it!"

I pulled the remaining coil off my shoulder and held it high above my head. I'd never been much good at throwing. I pulled back my arm and let it go. It flew through the air, uncoiling as it went, until it landed right in the boat and Mike grabbed it. Chuckie flashed me a thumbs-up sign and Mr. Amos bent down beside Mike, probably tying the rope down. I retreated to the beach. Before reaching land I passed by a dozen kids on the line, waiting. A bunch of them — some of them kids who wouldn't have said boo to me a few days before — congratulated me on the throw. I moved over to where Christina was holding the other end of the line.

"You ready?" I asked.

"Yeah."

"Make sure you don't pull until Mr. Amos signals it's okay," I cautioned.

"I know."

"And when the whale starts moving into the water you're going to have to go too, staying off to the side, getting ready to release it."

"I'm not an idiot, Gordon. I think I understand what I have to do!" she replied angrily.

"I didn't mean anything bad, I was just trying . . ." I didn't finish the sentence.

I wanted to walk away, but instead I stood silently beside her, looking out to the boat.

"I'm sorry," she said softly. "It's just that the whole thing depends on me. I tied the knot and I just hope it releases."

"I saw you tie it. It looked good."

"I just wish I'd checked it one more time to make sure it would release."

"Maybe we can check it before —"

My words were cut off by the high-pitched whine of the engine. A cloud of smoke rose from it as it worked furiously, but the boat stayed in place. All along the taut rope kids were pulling with all their might. The whale didn't seem to be budging. Its flippers were moving, though — thrashing through the air frantically. It didn't know we were trying to save it. All it could feel was the rope tightening around its tail, and hear the whine of the engine. It must have been terrified.

More kids rushed into the water and grabbed onto the line. I wanted to join them but felt that I needed to stay close to Christina . . . just in case.

"Come on . . . come on . . ." Christina pleaded.

As if in answer I saw, or thought I saw, the whale slide just a little toward the water.

"It's moving!" Christina screamed "It's moving!" She took a few tentative steps into the water.

I couldn't really tell, but I hoped and prayed she was right. A large wave broke on the beach and rolled up the shore, spraying against the tail of the whale. The water seemed to somehow grease the sand and the whale was drawn back in with the retreating wave. It was clear it was working, the whale was moving! Its whole body was almost in the water. The flippers were moving wildly, churning through the air and then the water. Despite its efforts to thwart the rescue it was still being pulled in.

Christina moved farther into the water. It was important that the line between her and the whale stayed slack. The least bit of tension and the knot would release and the whale would propel itself back onto the beach. I followed behind her as she waded into the swells.

Some of the kids on the end of the rope closest to the boat had to abandon their grip as the water became deeper. They shuffled down the line and took up places in shallower water. Christina was in the water almost up to her waist.

"Now! Now!" Mr. Amos yelled.

Kids let go of the rope at the same instant Christina pulled on her end, releasing the knot. Free, the whale surged forward toward the shore. We all held our breath and the whale swerved and turned away from the beach. It dipped under the water, with only its dorsal fin breaking the surface. It turned completely around and aimed itself out to the deep water. Kids scrambled to the side to try to escape from the oncoming whale. It rushed past them, expelled air, and then vanished as it hit deeper water.

Christina and I looked at each other in disbelief. It was gone. We both screamed in delight, screams that were being repeated dozens of times along the whole beach. I felt tears starting to form in my eyes — tears of joy — and I reached up and brushed them away. The salt water on my hands stung my eyes, and I thought I might cry for another reason.

A horn blasted and I spun around to see Mr. Amos waving his arms frantically in the air, trying to get my attention. Mike and Chuckie were feverishly pulling in the rope. I started wading toward the boat.

Mr. Amos moved to the rudder and turned the boat back toward shore. It circled and then made a pass in front of me. Mike heaved the rope into the air and it splashed down in the water beside me. I grabbed it and hustled back to the beach.

There were now eight whales part way in the water, on the line between shore and surf. As well, the corpse of one of the dead whales was being bashed around by the waves as it floated in the shallows. It was rocking with each wave and I was afraid the sheets would be washed off to reveal the shotgun blast to the head. There wasn't time to explain. There wasn't time for anything. It would soon be nightfall.

Christina had already picked the next whale to be rescued. It was one of a cluster of three; a medium-sized male and a larger female with a much smaller "baby" between them.

"Let's get the little one into the water," she said, taking the rope from my arms.

"No!" I objected. "It won't do any good. We'll free it and then it'll just swim back to be with its mother," I said, pointing to the female.

"Well . . . how about we free the mother first and then push in the baby?"

"That won't work either. I bet the mother will try to beach itself to get back to the baby," I countered.

"Then what do we do?" she asked anxiously.

"We can . . . we can . . . free them both at the same time," I reasoned.

"But how?"

"Tie the rope onto the female. Don't forget to put the sheets in place first. I'll get Ms. Fleming to organize a group to push the baby in. It can't weigh that much."

I explained things to Ms. Fleming. She quickly gathered up five kids who would push "Pudding" back into the water. During his time out of the water the brown colouring that had earned him his name had changed to a more greyish colour.

Christina called me back over. I grabbed the end of the rope and ran back out through the waves to get to the boat. Even though I hurled the end at the boat, it fell short. I was just going to go out after it when Mike dove over the side, gathered up the rope and swam back to the boat. He passed the rope over the side, and then Chuckie helped haul him back into the boat.

Kids, all those who weren't at Pudding's side, gathered along the length of the rope. Everybody wanted to be part of what was going to happen. After so much work, and so much frustration, they needed to be part of success.

Christina again moved to the side, holding the release end. I hurried back along the line, trying to get in position to help.

The engine revved noisily to signal that the operation had begun. This time there was an almost instant reaction. The large female started sliding back into the water. Quickly she was completely in the waist-deep water. She bucked wildly, her tail smashing the water and her flippers breaking the surface, fighting against our efforts. She was frantically trying to beach herself again.

I reached down to the rope, to lend a hand against her efforts, but looking past her I realized that Pudding was still on the beach. The five kids didn't seem to be able to dislodge her.

I turned to the kids on the line behind me.

"You, and you, and you two!" I yelled, "come with me."

One let go of the rope while the other three just gave me confused looks.

"Now!" I yelled. They dropped the rope. "Follow me!"

I splashed up the shore to Pudding. The little whale was whistling in terror.

"Everybody, get ready to push," I ordered. One boy was slow to respond and I grabbed him by the arm and pushed him into position.

"Wait for the wave . . . get ready . . . now!" I screamed.

The wave broke over the top of the whale, and as it receded the whale slid down with it.

"Go! Go! Go!" I yelled.

The whale hit the water and started swimming toward its mother, which was clearly in deep enough water to swim free. At the same instant Mr. Amos signalled for Christina to release the line. The big female surged forward and circled her baby, protecting it and then shepherding it toward the open water.

I stumbled back up the incline, along with the other kids who'd been pushing Pudding. I collapsed onto the sand and tucked in my arms and legs. I felt cold. The sun was now so low in the sky that the dunes on the edge of the beach were casting long shadows that extended to where I sat. Even more important than the tides, we didn't have much time left before the sun set.

"Are you okay, Gordon?" Ms. Fleming asked.

"Yeah . . . I guess so," I said as I got to my feet unsteadily.

"Let me go out and get the rope, you rest."

"I'm okay," I said weakly.

"Sit. Figure out which whale is next."

I sat back down on the sand as she ran into the water. Christina waded up the beach.

"We'll do the daddy whale next."

I slowly nodded my head in agreement. "We're not going to have time to do them all."

"Thank goodness we won't have to," she answered.

"What do you mean?"

"Didn't you notice? While we were putting those two back into the water, three of the others helped themselves. Look!"

I stood up and stared down the beach. Where there had been five whales there were now only two. And they seemed on the verge of freeing themselves, too.

"Wait here for Ms. Fleming to bring you back the rope. Tie it around the daddy whale."

I gathered up kids who were sitting or standing, waiting to pull in the next whale. There was an almost dream-like quality to things, and my legs and arms felt rubbery and weak. There was no time to wait for the rope to be brought back in. We had to act fast. If we could just turn them toward the water maybe we wouldn't need to tow them out.

"Come on, everybody!" I called out.

Others, sitting on the beach, rose and followed me to the first of the two whales bobbing in the surf. Quickly I divided the kids up so we could turn the whale around; half took positions along the tail while the other half lined up on the other side by the head. Rather than taking a position to push I yelled out orders and put people into their positions. On signal they pushed, and with the help of two large breaking waves the whale was turned around enough to move itself free of the beach. Its flippers and tail stroked powerfully and it vanished into the water.

Without a second of celebration people moved into position alongside the second whale and the whole process was repeated. With the rising tide, breaking waves and the desire of the whales to get back in the water, the task was easy. Soon the second whale was gone.

There were still seven whales left on the beach; the "daddy" of the three whales was almost completely submerged, three other whales were being touched by waves, and three more were still high and dry. As well, in the fading light I could see the corpses of Captain and two of the other dead whales, which remained out of the water. A second body had been met by the sea and was being bounced by the waves.

I glanced at my watch. It was 9:15. High tide and nightfall were both less than fifteen minutes away.

By now the boat was back in position and the line extended from the whale to the waiting boat. The spots along the rope were being filled by willing hands. I didn't feel like I had enough power left to help pull. Instead I moved over to where Christina stood, holding the release line.

"You look awful," she said.

"Thanks a lot."

"No, I mean you look really white . . . pale . . . and are you shaking?"

"I'm cold," I admitted reluctantly.

Before she could respond the engine of the boat started racing and everything else was forgotten.

This whale was practically in the water already and he easily slid back in completely. The whale turned sharply and started to parallel the shore, heading toward where Christina and I stood. It dipped its head beneath the waves and the gigantic flippers propelled it forward. The dorsal fin skimmed along the surface. With amazing speed it was coming right for us! I scrambled backwards in one direction and Christina did the same in the other. The whale shot between us. Christina stumbled backwards and disappeared under the water but almost instantly resurfaced.

"The rope! The rope!" she screamed.

For a split second I didn't realize what she meant, but then I saw the end of the line, the release end, free of her hand and being towed out by the whale. I struggled forward, hardly able to move through the chest-deep water. I planted my feet against the bottom and dove forward, my outstretched hands reaching for the fleeing line. I felt it running through my fingers, closed my hand, and then brought up the second hand to grip it. It snapped and then went slack. The whale was free.

There was a shrill blast of a whistle. Mrs. Murphy stood on the beach, up from the crest of the highest waves, and was calling out to us.

"What is she doing?" I gasped.

She blew on the whistle again.

"She wants us to come over to her I think," Christina said as she grabbed my arm. I felt so tired and weak I was grateful for her support, and together we slogged out of the water to join the gathering crowd. Exhausted, I slumped to take a seat on the sand. Everybody else seemed to be just as tired, and there was hardly a rumble of conversation as we waited for her to begin. She looked like she was trying to do a head count.

"Good," she began, "we're all here! We're going back up to the school now."

There was total and complete silence, as if we were all too stunned to believe what she had just said. Christina recovered and broke the silence.

"What do you mean? We can't go anywhere. There are still six whales to put back into the water."

Other kids shouted their agreement.

"No, I'm sorry, but Ms. Fleming and I have agreed it's far too dangerous for us to try to work in the dark."

"Our first priority is your safety," Ms. Fleming agreed. "We can't risk your lives."

"But you can't just give up!" a voice called out.

"We're not," Ms. Fleming responded. "I'll stay down here and work with Mr. Amos."

"The two of you can't do it alone," I protested. The words popped out so quickly they even caught me by surprise.

"He's right. You need all of us to help!" Christina agreed.

"We'll do the best we can. All of you should get up to the school before nightfall," Mrs. Murphy stated firmly.

Christina rose to her feet. I already knew what she was going to say.

"I'm not going up to the school. I'm staying here!"

"You'll do what you're told, young lady!" Mrs. Murphy objected.

"Christina, I know how you feel, how we all feel, but you have to listen. You have to go up to the school," Ms. Fleming interjected.

There was a blast of a horn. We all turned around. Mr. Amos was standing up frantically waving at us. He was yelling something, but I couldn't quite make out the words over the rush of the waves. I figured we were lucky we couldn't hear what he was saying. He was probably confused by us all stopping when there was still work to be done.

I rose to my feet and stood beside Christina. "I'm

not going either. Not until all the whales are back in the water."

All around us kids took to their feet. The boat's horn blasted out again and Mrs. Murphy started blowing her whistle and Ms. Fleming yelled for us all to sit down. And then I saw the white and red running lights of a large boat enter the bay.

"Here, I brought another round of hot chocolate for everybody," I said, putting the tray down on the table. People thanked me as they took the drinks.

"Feels good going down," Mike announced, taking a big slurp.

"Hold on!" Christina demanded, holding her cup aloft. "A toast . . . we need to have a toast. To us, we did it!"

I tipped my cup back. The chocolate tasted as wonderful as anything I'd ever tasted in my life.

"We did have some help, though," Mike added. "Not that we couldn't have done it by ourselves."

"Yeah, right," Chuckie piped up.

"But the whales were saved. That's what's important," Christina maintained.

It hadn't taken long for Dr. Resney, assisted by Mr. Amos, the crew of the ferry and the ferryboat itself, to put the remaining six whales back into the water. We'd all stayed on the beach and watched. The whole scene was illuminated by the big searchlights of the ferryboat. It was a strange feeling to watch them finish what we had started. Not that I wasn't grateful for their help, but it was a bittersweet feeling when the last of the whales disappeared into the water. If it hadn't been for the patches of linen littering the beach, and the dark, covered body of Captain still lying there, it all could have been nothing more than a dream.

While we were on the beach watching, the generator back at the school was being fixed. A technician had been brought along and he had it up and running before we got back. It was wonderful to be greeted by warm food and drink. It wasn't until my second bowl of soup and third cup of hot chocolate that my body stopped shaking.

Extra batteries had been brought from the ferry, and soon the radio was working as well. Dr. Resney made the first call out, to the Whale Stranding Network, so they could come out in the morning and examine the corpses of the dead whales. He said they'd be performing autopsies on the whales that might help scientists better understand what had happened to cause the stranding. He told us that maybe we could even witness the autopsies. I didn't know if I had the stomach for it or not, but I knew I couldn't be there to watch them cut open Captain. It just wouldn't have been right.

Next Mrs. Murphy insisted each one of us call home to our parents. Since we were allowed only one call, I had to think about whether to call my mother or father. I decided to call my mom. She sounded really grateful and relieved to hear my voice. At the end of the call I asked her to call my father and let him know I was okay too. She promised, even though I knew it would be hard for her to do; she hadn't called him since he'd left. Then, even more surprising, she said she'd even be polite if "what's her name" answered the phone.

She told me how worried all the parents had been and how the school had been inundated with calls from our families. The school had insisted that everything was all right but hadn't been able to provide any information. And because of all those calls, Dr. Resney was made to come out this evening to check on everybody rather than waiting for morning. I don't think he was too happy to have to leave his wife and newborn daughter, but he said, a dozen times, how happy he was now to have taken part in a whale rescue. He said between the birth of his child and the whale rescue this had been the most exciting day of his life.

"Well, time to turn in for the night!" Mike said unexpectedly. He rose from the table and then grabbed Chuckie by the arm, pulling him up.

"Good night everybody . . . and Gordo, don't stay up too late." Chuckie smiled.

"Why are you going to bed?" I asked. "Mrs. Murphy said we could stay up a little bit later."

"Need my beauty sleep," Mike replied.

"Sleep? Who said anything about sleep?" Chuckie asked. "The night is still young."

STRANDED

Mike gave him a shot in the arm. "Don't stay up too late, Gordo, we'll be waiting." They hurried down the hall.

There was an ominous tone to his voice when he said "we'll be waiting" that made me feel uneasy. I wondered what he meant . . . oh, no . . . I turned to Christina.

"They're going to do something to me tonight, aren't they?"

"They're always planning something," she answered.

"Great, just great! I can't believe they've still got it in for me, after all we've been through!"

"Take it as a compliment," Christina said.

"How can it be a compliment?"

"They mainly play jokes on people they like. But you don't have to worry."

"I don't?"

"You don't," she echoed.

"How can you be so sure?"

"Because of this." Christina reached over and dropped an empty plastic ring from a six-pack of pop onto the table.

My eyes widened. "Those aren't from Mike's Cokes, are they?"

"Yep."

"What happened to them?"

"We took them hostage. Christina had me slip in and get them about ten minutes ago," Lauren explained.

Stealing Mike's Cokes didn't strike me as a great

way to get him in a better mood. "And where are they now?" I asked anxiously.

"Safely hidden away someplace where Mike can't get them," Christina answered.

"Not unless he goes into my suitcase," Jenna giggled.

"But he's going to explode when he finds his Coke gone . . . he'll blame me. Why did you do it?" I demanded.

"So they'll leave you alone," Christina replied.

"Leave me alone? How is this going to get them to leave me alone?"

"Simple. Give this to Mike," Christina said, picking up the plastic ring and handing it to me. "Tell him you have his Cokes. If he wants to see any of them again he'd better leave you alone. Tell him one Coke will be delivered each morning if he agrees."

"Agrees! He'll agree to kill me!"

"No he won't," Christina reassured me. "And just to be sure, tell him you have a great idea about a trick to play on somebody and you won't tell him till morning."

"I don't have any ideas about a trick!" I protested.

"You don't need one. Tomorrow morning make them guess what your plan is. Wait till they guess something that sounds interesting and then tell them they guessed right."

"Would that really work?"

"Trust me," Christina replied.

"Come on, we'd better get to bed," Jenna said. Lauren got up from her seat.

"You two go ahead. I'll be there in a minute," Christina told them.

The two girls walked away, giggling to each other and looking back over their shoulders.

"They can be pretty goofy sometimes," Christina began. "But they are my friends . . . like you're my friend. We are friends, right?"

"Of course we're friends," I answered.

"But just friends . . . I hope you understand?" Christina asked.

"Yeah, sure." I felt relieved. And disappointed.

"After all, we're only twelve," she continued. "But who knows what'll happen in a few years."

"Who knows," I replied.

"See you in the morning," she said.

I watched her walk away and disappear down the girls' corridor. She was right, who knows what'll happen in a few years.

I picked up the ring-tab. I guess it was time to see if it would work. I looked around the room. It was almost empty. Mr. Amos sat at the front with Dr. Resney. He saw me and motioned for me to come over.

"You done good out there, Gordon."

"Thanks . . . but we couldn't have done it without you."

"I guess I didn't do bad for an old man," he agreed.

"Not bad?" Dr. Resney answered. "Pretty amazing is how I'd describe it."

Mr. Amos just smiled. He looked like the cat that swallowed the canary.

"And who would have thought those two in the

boat with me, one as bald as a billiard ball and the other with green hair, could have done such a good job? Good kids they are."

"Yeah, they are . . . both of them," I agreed.

"And young Christina! What a trooper, a real fighter. Reminds me a lot of my wife, my Christina. You got yourself quite a girlfriend there."

"She's not my . . ." I stopped and smiled. "Thanks."

"And there's even better news," continued Dr. Resney, "Mr. Amos has agreed to offer some assistance for the rest of the week. I'll certainly need all the help I can get in the absence of my wife."

"You're going to work here?" I asked in amazement, remembering what Mrs. Presley had said about how he felt about the school.

"Pretty shocking, isn't it?" He cackled and took a sip from his coffee.

"An offer should have been made before this," Dr. Resney said. "It's going to be wonderful."

"Don't know if it'll be wonderful," Mr. Amos cautioned. "I don't know nothing about teaching or any fancy talk, but I have eighty years' worth of stories I can tell."

"Make that eighty years' worth of knowledge about the sea. Those whales wouldn't have made it without you," Dr. Resney corrected him.

"Don't forget the kids . . . especially this one and Christina."

"Nobody will be forgetting them, believe me. The Stranding Network has already contacted the newspapers. This story will be carried all over

North America, maybe even the world. You're all going to be heroes! . . . Oh, my gosh, that reminds me, I'd better radio over to my wife. She doesn't know about any of this, and if she hears it from the news reports before she hears it from me she'll kill me."

Dr. Resney rose from the table, leaving the two of us alone.

"I'm glad you're going to be around this week. Maybe you could even talk to other groups after ours," I suggested.

"Maybe. Haven't been asked, and besides, I might not like it."

"I guess we'll find out." I paused. "Could I ask you a question?"

"Sure."

"What made you change your mind and come and help us?"

"I never did change my mind."

"What do you mean?"

"I always was going to help."

"You were always going to help, even though you were a whaler?"

"'Course I was. A long time ago I killed whales for a living . . . to feed my family and put a roof over their heads. I didn't do it for pleasure or because I hated them. All those years at sea I learned lots of things, and one of those was respect for life. Those whales on the beach needed my help if they were going to live. There was nothing to gain in letting them die. Do you understand?"

"I guess . . . sort of, but you were so angry at us I didn't think you'd help."

"Course I was mad at you! I still am angry! Darn fool kids nearly scared me to death!" he thundered, and the few remaining people in the dining room turned toward us.

"But we didn't mean anything bad, honestly. We just didn't know," I apologized again.

"I know, I know," he replied quietly, and his expression softened. "And I knew that just because I was angry at you kids that didn't give me the right to do the wrong thing."

"What do you mean?" I asked.

"You know what they say, 'two wrongs don't make a right.' Ever hear that before?" he asked.

"Yeah, I think. Could I ask you one more question?"

He turned his wrist over and looked at his watch. "It's getting late. One last question."

"There wasn't a choice, you had to kill those whales, didn't you?"

"What do you think?"

"You had no choice," I answered.

"If you knew, then why'd you ask?"

"I don't know . . . I guess I just wished there was some way we could have saved them all."

"So did I, but wishing don't make something so. Sometimes you just have to look at the cards you're dealt and play them the best way you can. We did the best we could out there, the very best."

"Yeah, I guess we did."

He stood up and leaned on his cane.

"Was a long day. I gotta go home and get some sleep before tomorrow. You planning on doing any more late-night visiting tonight?"

"No, I'm going to sleep!"

"Glad to hear that. I'll see you in the morning."

"Good night, Mr. Amos."

Slowly, leaning on his cane, he walked across the dining room and out the door. I took a last sip of cold hot chocolate. I felt a wave of tiredness sweep over me, and my thoughts turned to my house and my room and lying in my bed snuggled under the covers with Sammy under my head, and my parents downstairs, getting ready to go to bed. And then I remembered how my room wasn't my room any more and my house didn't belong to us any more, and most important, how my parents lived apart. I felt a rush of anger and then a sudden release. Maybe it was time for me to try to make the best of what I had instead of wishing for something that wasn't going to happen. Maybe it was time to try to make things easier for everybody, or at least try not to make things more difficult.

But first things first. I pulled the plastic pop ring out of my pocket. This wasn't perfect either, but maybe I could make it work . . . at least enough so I could get to sleep tonight.